THE HORSEHEAD TRAIL

When Charlie Goodnight leaves the Texas Rangers all he wants is to raise enough cash to marry his girlfriend. He's got a herd of longhorns to sell, but instead of driving them north to Kansas, he heads south-west into a land no white man has ever taken a herd before. They tell him he is crazy. This is dangerous Comanche country and he will have to blaze a trail across a waterless desert. The odds are all against him. But only time will tell . . .

JOHN DYSON

THE HORSEHEAD TRAIL

Complete and Unabridged

LINFORD
Leicester

First published in Great Britain in 1999 by
Robert Hale Limited
London

First Linford Edition
published 2000
by arrangement with
Robert Hale Limited
London

British Library CIP Data

Dyson, John, *1943 –*
    The Horsehead Trail.—Large print ed.—
    Linford western library
    1. Western stories
    2. Large type books
    I. Title
    823.9'14 [F]

    ISBN 0–7089–5683–1

Published by
F. A. Thorpe (Publishing) Ltd.
Anstey, Leicestershire

Set by Words & Graphics Ltd.
Anstey, Leicestershire
Printed and bound in Great Britain by
T. J. International Ltd., Padstow, Cornwall

This book is printed on acid-free paper

1

It all began when a Mexican asked me if I wanted to buy fifty cows. We were sitting at the counter of a cantina in the West Texas town of Freedom and up to that point all I had said to him was, 'Mister, pass me that Grizzly Bear relish.' He had complied with a friendly mouthful of tacos and flashing teeth; a cheerful bow-legged little cuss in tight studded leathers, his sombrero on his back, his head as bald, brown and shiny on top as a conker, rats' tails hanging down around.

'What in hell would I want with fifty cows?'

'Señor, you drive them up to the Kansas railroad you get a good price for them.'

'Ha! Don't make laugh. A thousand miles, cross seven major rivers, through Indian Territory, for *fifty* cows?'

'You can make it, *hombre*.'

I almost choked on my mess of *enchiladas* and fried eggs trying to control my laughter. 'You're crazy. To make any money a man needs to take two or three thousand up there.'

'So,' he shrugged, 'sell my fifty for a profit in Texas. I let you have them chee-eep.'

I tipped some relish on my black eye beans and stirred it in. They were already spiced with chilli, but us Texans like our food like our women — red hot. And we find it hard to resist scoring a point, especially over our southern neighbours. 'What do you call cheap?'

'You know anything about cattle?'

'Not a lot.' It didn't seem necessary to tell him I was part-owner with my step-brother in a herd of 5,000. 'I ain't been mustered out the Rangers long.'

'Rangers? Texas Rangers?' He gave me a slanty look. 'These ain't stole, *señor*.'

'Then how you come by 'em?'

2

'I just pick them up. They got no brand. There are many thousands of them — you call long-horns — running wild out there. But fifty is all I can drive on my own.'

I chewed on my enchiladas some more, a bead of sweat running off my nose. They sure were hell hot. 'What you mean out there, *hombre*?'

'Up along the San Saba River, and Green Mounds.'

'That Comanche country? You rode through there alone?'

'*Si*, I got to. My mother, my sister, we live at Presidio del Norte on the Rio Grande. I cross the wide table lands to the Rio Pecos, and along the Horsehead Trail.'

'The Horsehead Trail? That's ninety-six miles without water. You came along that?'

'*Si*, I keep my horse at a hard run. It only take me two nights.'

'That's fast. You see any Comanche?'

'No, the Horsehead Trail too desolate for them. They mainly further north

3

on the *Llano Estacado* and the Salt Plains.'

'That's dangerous country, nonetheless.' I was beginning to have a new respect for this little guy. As I say, I had done my war service in the Rangers protecting the border settlers from Comanche. They had got uppity, raiding and looting the farms left behind by the men who went away to fight for the Rebel cause. And we Rangers rarely ventured far into those half-explored lands unless we had a posse of a dozen. 'OK. Where are these cows?'

'I put them in the town corral. It is empty. How about it? You geev me two dollar a head?'

'If they're running wild along the Saba why do I need to pay for them? One dollar.'

'*Muy bien.*' He put out his greasy paw and shook mine. 'Now I can pay for my meal.'

I took my roll from my shirt pocket and peeled off fifty dollars. 'How would you like to work for me?'

'Work for you?' He gave a shrill giggle. 'You wan' tequila?'

'Nope.' I guess I didn't look like the employer type in my faded blue canvas shirt, red bandanna, torn *chaparreras*, and worn high-heel boots. The serving girl was passing a bowl of coffee my way, and taking my plate. 'Just slide that jug of cream along, *amigo*.'

Since the war ended, Confederate currency, with which I had just paid my friend, was as worthless as dried leaves. One good dollar a longhorn was ridiculous, but it was half the price they were going for in Texas. Folks down here hadn't cottoned on fully to their worth as beef and they were still being rendered down for hides and tallow for candles. If a man wanted to make real money, Yankee money, out of beeves he had to drive them north to Kansas. Or, perhaps, I had been thinking, there was another market?

'Hey.' I rolled a cigarette and tossed my tobacco pouch to the Mex. 'Do you reckon you could drive cows along that Horsehead Trail to Horsehead Crossing on the Pecos?'

'Not unless you crazy in the head.' He twirled himself a quirly, and lit up. 'Half them die of thirst. Anyhow, where you drive them?'

'New Mexico.'

He grinned. 'Now I know you crazy.'

I smiled back, for he had a point. 'There's eight thousand Navajo Indians held on the reservation up there. There's a government contract to supply them with beef.'

'There is?' he laughed. 'You don' say?'

'I do say. That's why I'm asking if you want to work for me? We'll round up these free-ranging longhorns out of the chapparal and trail them up.'

'How much you pay?'

'The going rate for a 'puncher. Twenty dollars a month. Yankee dollars. Paid at the end of the trail. May be a twenty dollar bonus if we do well.'

6

'*Si*? Sound OK.' He threw back his purple-striped *serape* and revealed a Dragoon revolver stuck in his leather belt. 'Maybe not OK.'

'That's the chance we take.' I exhaled smoke and stubbed the cigarette. 'To tell the truth I've been kidding you. I've already got two thousand cows. I got mustered out the Rangers early and since then I've been in partnership with my step-brother. We own the CV ranch out on the Palo Pinto prairie. But me and JW we've had a falling out. He told me to take my half of the cows and go. So, that's what I'm gonna do.'

'But, what about your ranch?'

'Aw, I told him to keep it. The South's in ruins. Land is practically worthless in Texas these days.'

'*Señor*, you are saying' — he waggled a finger at me — 'you wan' me to work for nothing for one, maybe two months, on your say-so you pay me at the end of that time? Are you still joking with me?'

7

'Nope. You would have to trust me.'

'Trust you? Why should I trust a gringo?'

'Because I used to be a Ranger, and because I'm a man of my word, and because I hate liars, hypocrits and thieves as much as I hate Comanches and *comancheros*.'

'You theenk I am *comanchero*?' he grinned. 'You theenk I am *bandido*?'

'Nope. I didn't say that. There are good greasers and bad uns. Something tells me you're a good one.'

'You don' say? Well, there's mighty few good greengos. But, you — OK, *señor*, I work for you.'

'Call me Charlie.' I stuck my Lone Star hat on my head and picked up my Spencer seven shot. I tossed another blotchy Confederate bill down on the counter and the owner, Manuel, gave an unhappy grimace as he studied it. 'Keep the change,' I said.

The Mexican jumped up and pumped my hand again. I'm a six-footer and he came up to my chest. 'My name it is Jesus Gerrigueta de Peyera,' he said.

'Quite a mouthful. Hang around.'

* * *

The reason why I hadn't stayed on in the Rangers was that since the collapse of the War of Rebellion a horde of Northern army blue-bellies had come riding in telling us how we ought to run things in Texas. I just didn't fancy taking orders from some fancypants captain from Boston. I wanted to be my own man. And the other reason was financial. Although me and JW had sold a few cows we had never really made much money, and what we had we had frittered away in the saloons on whiskey, gambling and dancing with the prairie nymphs. I was kicking thirty. I had sown my wild oats. I wanted to make something of myself, marry and settle down.

And there was, perhaps, another, a

most important reason: I knew who I wanted to marry. I'd been smitten. The love bug. That old black magic, romance, Cupid's arrow, call it what you will. But it had proved more deadly than any Comanche's. Mary Ann was her name. The sweetest li'l chickadee I had ever set eyes on. That's why I was hanging around this town called Freedom. Her daddy owned Pfout's Emporium, the general store. Unfortunately, he had a high opinion of himself, and a low one of me.

Freedom was about the furthest you could go in West Texas and be reasonably sure of hanging on to your hair. But most of the store-keepers seemed puffed up by the idea it was the centre of civilization. Yes, Mary Ann and I had the hots for each other. It was her daddy who was the bugbear.

'If you think I'm going to allow my daughter to consort with some saddlebum former Texas Ranger who all he has to his credit is a revolver, a belt of bullets and a horse, you've got another think coming.' Those were his words. And, in a way, I didn't blame him. He wanted a decent future for his daughter. And I did, too.

2

Mary Ann was reigning over her father's emporium, sitting straight-backed in a modest frilled blouse with cameo at the throat, and a tight-waisted long skirt, in the raised-up cash box at the rear of the store. 'Hi,' she called, fluttering her fingers to me. 'You come to ask me to go to the barbecue tonight?'

'Sho' have, my li'l darlin',' I said, because we were on familiar terms by this time.

'Well, seems like you left it too late 'cause Gideon Claypole came by and asked me for the honour of being his dancing companion.' Mary Ann gave a haughty sniff of her little pointed nose and returned to studying the accounts. 'And, seein' as you hadn't showed I accepted him.'

'Huh!' I growled, for if there's one thing I can't abide and that's a man with a queer religious name. And the next is a lawyer. And Gideon Claypole qualified on both those counts. 'That dang stuffed shirt?'

Mary Ann had asked me not to bother her in the store, on account of it got her daddy over on the meat counter raging mad, so that was the reason why I hadn't come in earlier. 'There's no need to be uncomplimentary about Mr Claypole,' she snorted, and dinged her finger on one of the keys of the big ornate till as she paid out change to a lady customer.

Mary Ann's cashier's box was built of polished wood, raised up like the preacher's pulpit in church, above the rows of shelves displaying all kinds of goodies, from bottles of bull's eyes, to boxes of bullets. There were dummies with ladies' hats and dresses, sacks of dried fruits, barrels of gunpowder, and tubs of molasses. When I first saw her I thought she was Queen Boadicea in her chariot, and maybe that's how I was so smitten.

That impression was re-inforced by the fact that instead of paying for their purchases at the four different counters, folks had to climb up steps to the cash box while the assistants wrote down what they owed, stuffed the note into a big cartridge, and, triggering the mechanism of a newfangled machine, sent it flying along a wire. Mary Ann calmly received the cartridge, entered its contents into a ledger, and accepted payment. How this simplified store-keeping I ain't sure, but it certainly looked good.

I touched my hat to her father, blood-faced and portly in a striped apron and straw hat, but he slammed his cleaver into a side of bacon and pretended to ignore me. However, I saw him scribble words onto a piece of paper, stuff it into a cartridge and whizz it away along the wire.

'What's he got to say this time?' I asked, friendly-like, an elbow on the ledge of her peephole.'

'Tell that no-good bastard to get

his ass out of my shop,' Mary Ann said aloud as she perused his epistle. 'Tell him you've had enough of him pestering you.'

'Tell him I've as much right to pester you as Gideon Claypole,' I said, my dander up. 'Tell him I'm a grown man and you're a grown woman.'

'I ain't that growed,' Mary Ann said, huffily, but wrote it all down and sent the cartridge speeding back along the wire like a bolt from her chariot.

Why her father corresponded with me in this manner I was never quite sure. Maybe he just wanted to be offhand and ornery, or did not feel he should deign to address me man to man. Or, maybe the hip-slung brace of Colt revolvers I wore on each thigh over my batwing chaps, the Spencer seven-shot under my arm, deterred him from insulting me directly.

Anyhow, he received the message, and his bullneck glowed even redder, if that was possible, as he slammed the cleaver clean through the bacon. 'Damn no good Ranger,' he shouted.

Mary Ann's prim little cupid-bow mouth pursed in a smile, and her funny-coloured eyes met mine. When I say she was full-grown I mean she was all of twenty-five. Some folks might have said an old maid and on the shelf. But to me she was just right, a vision of loveliness. Her hair, I suppose, was what they call dun-coloured, and scraped back into a bun, but that accentuated the strong bone structure of her noble head.

'He don't seem to like me,' I muttered.

'That's just 'cause he thinks you're only after my body,' Mary Ann cooed, fluttering her eyelashes. 'Or his money.'

'That's a dastardly thing to think,' I protested, although privately and guiltily I had to admit the memory of Mary Ann sitting there filled my night thoughts with dreadful fantasies.

'Daddy says you ain't got a hundred dollars to rub together an' you never will have. Whereas, he says that Gideon Claypole is a go-getter and this town's future leading citizen.'

'And I guess he's told you to grab him while you can. Well, Mary Ann, that's your privilege,' I said, glumly, 'but I've just stepped in to tell you I've split with my step-brother, Mr Steeck. And I'm moving my cattle out. I'm taking 'em where no man's never taken a herd before. Not in known history. Not, at least, a white man. If you'll just hang on for me a couple of months or more, I'll be back with cash in my belt. Yankee cash. And I'll be here to ask your hand in marriage.'

'Sonuvabitch, Charlie, you say the durndest things,' Mary Ann drawled, fanning herself with an accounts sheet. 'You make me come all over faint. What the heck's this no man's trail you're going on?'

'That's my secret, Mary Ann. The world will know one day.'

'Listen to him,' her father roared

from his counter. He scribbled some more for his cartridge and hastily fired it in our direction. I guess it was like a substitute six-gun.

'Cattle is tiddly-winks in Texas,' Mary read out. 'Or any place else. The man's crazy. Dump him.'

'Tell him I'm going, darlin',' I said. 'And tell him I'll be back for you.'

★ ★ ★

I shaved with my cut-throat razor, scraped back my hair with axle grease, gave my boots their monthly polish, and tied on a new lilac bandanna, so was feeling quite the Jack o'Dandy when I strolled out after dark to the circle of wagons inside which a bonfire glowed. Folks had come by buggy and wagon from neighbouring farms far and wide for the barbecue. They might have lost the war, and they might not have much cash, but that didn't stop them having fun. Some were already prancing about on the raised platform,

18

screaming like Comanches as fiddles thrummed.

Imagine my fury when I saw Gideon Claypole up there with Mary Ann, swinging her round by the waist like he was her regular beau. He had pipped me to the post again. 'Birdie hop out and crane hop in, three hands round and go it again,' the leathery-lunged caller intoned, as Mary Ann and Claypole split up and sashayed back to their opposite lines. She stood there smiling and clapping among the women as some other girl skipped forward to be swung around like a bag of meal by a burly rustic. Then it was their turn again. 'Meet your partner and all chaw hay, dozee-do and take her away.' And with a whoop Mary Ann went waltzing and spinning back and forth in Claypole's arms.

I spat my cigar into the dust with disgust and moved over to the punchbowl on its bench. 'Come on, I need a drink,' I said to the Mexican with the high-falutin' name.

'I theenk that *señorita* geev me the eye,' Jesus grinned, as our glasses were filled. 'She got a face like a horse, but — whoopa! — what a body.' He clenched his fist and waved it under my nose. 'I theenk this gonna be my lucky night.'

I turned and saw Mary Ann smiling as she waited at the edge of the stage. She gave me her little teasing wave. 'You watch your mouth and take your eyes offen her. That's the woman I love.'

'Thass so? Well, maybe she don' look so much like a horse. I was only jokin', *amigo*.'

'Look at that dandy she's with,' I said, as Claypole joined her, proffering a glass of punch. 'Look at that celluloid collar and city suit. Damn jackanapes.'

Mary Ann frowned and strolled over to introduce him. 'I don't think you've met Mr Claypole.'

'Thass all right, I know who he is,' I muttered, ignoring his outstretched hand. 'One thing's for sure, I know when a town's got too dang civilized for its own good, when it's time to move on to pastures new, that's when the hypocrits arrive.'

'What do you mean by that, sir?' Claypole asked.

'I mean when they build a church and pay for a mealy-mouthed preacher to tell us how to behave. I mean when lawyers arrive like a cloud of lousy vultures to pick at people's bones.'

'Don't take any notice of him, Gideon,' Mary Ann soothed. 'Charlie's just jealous, thassall.'

'Wasn't Gideon the one in the Bible who had three score and ten sons. You're gonna be kept busy, Mary Ann.'

'Maybe I am,' she smirked, as she turned Claypole away towards the barbecue.

I watched them out of the corner of my eye, seething as they cut their steaks, and chatted, and ate, and went back to the dancing. What riled me most was that he wasn't a bad-looking feller and, a fancy stepper, cut quite a dash. The wooden floor was pounding and fury imbued the whole affair as the Texans, full of life and raw spirits, did what they loved to do best, swing their partners. 'First lady to the left, do the same again . . .'

I stood there glum and alone with my drink for company, for Jesus had found himself a little farmer's daughter and was sashayin her, as well. So, I wandered off into the darkness. When I returned around the back of a wagon an arm came out and hooked me around the throat, pulling me back. My hand instinctively went for one of my guns.

'You durn fool, you could get yourself killed. I thought you was a Comanch,' I said.

'No, I'm not a damned Comanch,' Mary Ann giggled, as she stuck her tongue down my throat, and we got ourselves glued tight.

'Where's Claypole?' I asked, as I came up for a breather.

'Aw, I told him I had to go some place,' Mary Ann said, and tightened her bony arm around my neck.

'Durn popinjay.'

'Aw, Claypole's OK. But it's you I like, Charlie.'

We set to seeking each other's lips and kissing some more like we were the first to have invented it, and Mary Ann was gasping and breathing hard, and getting hold of my hand and pressing it on to her breast. Sometimes I had the idea she wasn't as innocent as she said she was.

'I'm settin' out first light. I cain't stand this what you're doin' to me, Mary Ann. I gotta go prove to your daddy I'm a worthy man.'

'Aw that ole curmudgeon. Why don't I go with you, Charlie? We'll elope.'

'No, we can't do that. A cattle drive ain't no honeymoon. There ain't no place on it for a gal. You wait for me, Mary Ann. I'll be back by the end of the year. I'll be rich.'

'That's more'n three months away.

Iffen you think I'm sittin' on my butt twiddlin' my thumbs while you're friggin' about with some lousy cows . . . '

Mary Ann could be very outspoken. Maybe that's what I liked about her.

3

We took our fifty cows from the town corral and headed back into the Palo Pinto towards my step-brother's ranch. It was just runty sagebrush scrubland and *en route* we were able to add another 200 to our herd by scouring the back ravines.

When the Texans went off to do their bit, or in many cases, give their all for the Confederacy, the longhorns had run wild and multiplied. In fact, someone estimated that there were five million longhorns in Texas after the war, undriven, untended, and mostly unbranded. It was these mavericks that me and Jesus Gerrigueta de Peyera scooped up as we went along.

'In Mexico the big landowners been making money from cattle for years. You Texans only just cottoned on to it?'

'Yeah, but I'm gonna make big money, too.'

'How about me? Twenty dollar a month ain't beeg.'

'Aw, come on, Jesus. We gotta get one thing straight: I'm the boss; you're just my *vaquero*. If you don't like it you can go.'

'I stay,' he sighed, sitting his mustang and peering down into a ravine where he had spotted a clutch of longhorns peacefully grazing. 'Hey, how about those babies?'

I nudged my liver-and-cream, shaggy-maned paint, Paddy, down the slope. 'Let's go get 'em, boy.'

It was a fine excitement to go charging down into the ravine, yipping and hollering, leaping the broncs over fallen cactii and swerving through great eroded rocks, cracking my coiled lariat to send the longhorns hightailing away before us in a cloud of dust.

I had been raised on the River Brazos and what you might call born in the saddle. My step-brother, J W Steeck, and I had 'learned cow' working on our neighbour's ranch as 'punchers, which, of course, included the arts of roping, pony racing, bull whacking and busting mustangs. In fact he allowed us to keep every fourth calf that was born so even as teenagers, we had a small bunch of about 200 to call our own. So I was no novice at the game. But anybody can make a mistake.

Maybe my newfound ambition to get those dollar signs ringing up made me forget caution, but when I saw a cow and her calf go charging up a narrow box canyon I spurred Paddy in after her. My leather *chaparerras* and boot *tapaderas* took the brunt of the thorn scrub and I shielded my face with an arm as barbed branches came slashing back at me. I went dashing through and suddenly found myself at the end of the canyon with the cow backed up in front of her calf and swinging her huge horns menacingly. A cow can be far more dangerous than a bull in such a situation, and this one was pawing the ground, her malevolent eyes, and the sharp-as-sword-tips horns aimed at me. Before I could get out of danger she was coming at me. There was barely room to manoeuvre in the narrow space, but I was lucky that my pinto had good 'cow sense'. He, desperately and nimbly, leapt aside as she charged. One of her horns tore through my chap. A half-inch closer and she would have taken off my leg. But I was not out of it yet. I was between her and her calf and she wouldn't like that. I turned the pinto to face her and she was coming back at me. At that moment, I was at a loss what the hell to do.

She was almost upon me when I heard Jesus crashing through the bush behind her, glimpsed his lariat spinning, saw its loop land over her horns and, at the split second she went to gouge the pinto's side, the Mexican took the strain with his saddle horn, there was a loud popping sound, and the cow took a somersaulting dive into the dirt.

I quickly rounded up the calf and sent it skittering to her as she clambered back up from her knees much chastened. Yelling and slapping we sent them running back to the main herd.

'Whoo!' I gave a whistle of relief. 'That was a close encounter. Thanks, *amigo*.'

The bald Mexican, with the fringe of hair around the back of his head hanging down to his purple serape, grinned at me. 'Never ride blind into a box canyon like that, Charlie.'

'Yeah, I shoulda knowed. I was carried away by the heat of the chase.'

'*Andale* gringo,' he called. 'Let's get after 'em.'

As we did so, I thought that at least I knew that here was a man who could handle cows and, I figured, could be relied on in an emergency.

★ ★ ★

The way that herd was growing, as we went rolling along day after day like

29

the tumbling tumbleweed, I began to realize that it was getting too big for the two of us. We would have to think about hiring some help. But where were we going to recruit them in this wilderness?

We had made camp at a muddy waterhole which we had located by watching some swallows carrying mud for nest building in their mouths and followed the direction from which they had flown, one of the signs you soon learn on the frontier. We were dog-tired as we cooked jack-rabbit on a spit, and roasted flapjack in the ashes, as the sun disappeared over the horizon, casting its crimson afterglow, and there began the eerie howls of the night-hunting critters.

'You know why they call 'em mavericks?' I was saying. 'After old Sam Maverick down on the San Antonio river. He neglected his branding and after a year of ranching found himself with very few cows left. His neighbours had made off with the unmarked ones.'

'That so, Charlie?' Jesus said, as he poured thick black coffee from our jug into tin cups and handed me one. 'Seems to me like we findin' two or three mavericks to every branded one.'

'Yeah, and some of those other brands ain't very clear so I guess there's no harm me putting mine over . . . ' My words trailed out as I saw the dark silhouettes of three horsemen riding towards us from out of the crimson dusk. I laid my coffee aside and reached for my seven-shot Spencer carbine as the hair at my nape tingled. They were not Comanches, but, with widebrimmed hats like that, they might well be *comancheros*. 'We got company.'

'*Si, señor*, I seen them,' Jesus hissed, drawing his long-barrelled Dragoon revolver from his belt and cocking it as he kneeled by the fire.

The three riders got closer and closer without making any sound, obviously attracted like moths to our firelight. And they were almost upon us, forty paces away, when I rose and shouted out, 'Hombres! Hold it right there! What's your business?'

The one in the centre gave a harsh ringing laugh as he reined in. He had a patch over one eye, and pale beard beneath a campaign hat pulled low over his brow. His good eye glittered forcibly, as he drawled, 'That coffee sure smells good. You got a cup to spare?'

'I asked who you was? What brings you here?'

'We ain't nobody much,' he said, with a wolfish grin. 'Jest weary, hard-done-by soldiers headin' home.'

'Yeah?' I eyed the bullet-holed skirts of his dusty grey Confederate topcoat. 'Well, maybe you'd better pass on by as quietly as you can without disturbing our cows. We ain't fond of company.'

'Aw, is that any way to talk to a veteran who's been away four years fighting to protect his countryfolk?'

There was something about the mean-jawed varmint that told me it might be best to send him on his way. Nor was I much taken by the hard looks of the shoddily clad 'ex-soldiers' who rode with him. But, hell, hadn't they been fighting in the war? Didn't I owe them some debt of gratitude? Sure, I had been in hard fighting with Comanche to protect my country folk, too, but somehow that didn't have the same ring to it.

I glanced at Jesus and said, 'Step down and join us.' But, as they did so, I kept my Spencer aimed vaguely in their direction.

They hunkered down around the fire and supped at the coffee Jesus passed them as the first stars flickered bright in the clear Texan sky.

'Had any trouble with Indians?' the one-eyed man asked.

'No, not recently. Since we gave the Comanch's a thrashing on the Pirandelles River they stay mainly out on the Staked Plains to the northwest. Our repeating carbines and revolvers kinda surprised them.'

'Yeah?' His good eye glinted as he regarded me. 'Who's us?'

'The Rangers.'

'You a Ranger?'

'I was. Served through the war.'

'Huh!' He gave a scoffing high-pitched laugh. 'You call that war service? You shoulda been at Shiloh. The dead fell so thick you had to climb over 'em. You hear that, boys? A few lousy Comanches he thinks he's a hero.'

'Well, they didn't give me no medals. But I guess somebody had to look after things back here.'

'Look after things? What, help yourself to other folks' cattle while they're away doing their duty?' His cynical laughter rang out again as he tossed the dregs of his coffee into the fire and pitched the tin cup back on to the sand before me. He turned and looked at the lowing herd drinking their fill at the waterhole. 'Looks to me like you're doing OK for yourself.'

'These were all unbranded stock,' — I

avoided saying 'nearly all', and waved my Spencer at them — 'if you're trying to say these were dishonestly come by you had better take a look at them for yourselves. And then apologize. I don't take those sort of insults from no man, ex-soldier or not.'

Jesus began to back away, his revolver ready, gripped in both his hands. I jerked up the Spencer at the bearded man's chest and said, 'You had better eat your words, or prepare to defend them.'

The two weatherbeaten war-rats glanced anxiously at their leader, and began to get to their feet.

'Aw, come on,' he said, flashing a crafty grin. 'Can't you take a joke? Who cares where you got the cows? Tell you one thing, mister, they sure ain't gonna hang around here you start shootin' that gun.'

I was hopping mad at this man's words and attitude, and ready to plug him then and there. He would go first, if I didn't manage to get the other two, and I told him so. But he just squatted there and made no move for his sidearm, wheedling his way out of it. I had no wish to stampede the hard-gathered herd so I tried to simmer down.

'Where are you fellas headed to?' I said. 'For if I was you I'd just keep headin' right on.'

'Listen to him,' the one-eyed man laughed. 'He's a real banty rooster, ain't he? I told you that's the way they are in Texas — always ready to go for their guns.'

'Yeah,' I muttered angrily. 'You better believe that. You didn't answer my question.'

'We ain't headed nowhere,' he grinned. 'We're from Arkansas, but the war's given us a taste for wanderin'. We're down on our luck and could do with a bite to eat if you've anything to spare. We're looking to find ourselves honest work on one of the spreads, thasall.'

'You are, are you?' I said. 'Well,

if you shoot your mouth like that you won't stay alive long in these parts, Shiloh or no Shiloh. Your war experiences don't cut no ice with us.'

'OK, mister, I'm sorry,' he replied, spreadeagling his hands, one of which had a finger missing, across the blaze. 'We got off on the wrong foot.'

It seemed to me he was some kind of yellow-bellied cuss to apologize so readily for his mouth. But, on the other hand, maybe I'd been too hot. 'There's what's left of that rabbit and some flapjack if you want to chaw on it.'

They did so, voraciously, like they hadn't eaten for a day or two. 'How do two of you manage to herd all these damn cows?' the one-eyed Jack asked between mouthfuls.

'With difficulty,' I said.

'Where you going?'

'Back to Freedom, then we're pushing west.'

'You need any help? We could do with a job.'

'Maybe.' I glanced at Jesus but he

wasn't saying anything. I certainly didn't like the look of these three hard men. But, out here a man couldn't be too choosy about who he employed. The labour market had been greatly depleted by the war. It was going to be difficult to sign up many cowboys for the big trail.

'Let's get this straight before we start. These cows are mine, the hub of my outfit. If I take you on as drovers there'll be no arguments. You do as I say. You don't quit. You get paid when we reach our destination and I've sold the herd. Twenty dollars a month, maybe a twenty dollar bonus at the end of the trail, depending on what I make. All I provide until then is our food and ammunition.'

The frock-coated Confederate adjusted his eye-patch and spat a piece of rabbit bone into the fire. 'Sounds OK to me. How about you boys?' His *compadres* shrugged, sourfaced, as if they were used to him making the decisions. 'Right. We're on. The name's Abel

Hagerty. This here's Slim Watson and this' — he hooked his thumb at the other — 'Jesse Wayne.'

I spat on my palm and slapped theirs across the fire. There was no friendship in the eyes I met, but I guessed they had had a hard time in the war. At the back of my mind I was telling myself I was a fool to take them on. Maybe they deserved a chance? Or maybe I was too soft-hearted? As we settled down around the fire and passed the tobacco I knew I would have to ride them hard and watch them like a hawk.

'Tomorrow we go pick up two thousand cows from the CV ranch,' I told them, as I went to take first watch with Slim over the herd, 'Then we'll drift back towards Freedom picking up any more strays as we go. I'll give you a day's rest and then we hit the trail.'

'Any good-lookin' gals in Freedom?' Haggerty asked. 'I ain't had a nice bit of muslin in a long time.'

'There is a real li'l firecracker.' Jesus

kissed his thumb and forefinger to the stars. 'Eyes like sage. And hair like ... like my pony's. But she belongs to the boss.'

'Yeah,' I growled, 'if that lawyer Claypole ain't got his claws in her by now.'

'You can never trust a woman. Nor a lawyer.' Hagerty gave his hyena laugh that was already beginning to annoy me, and made an obscene remark. 'I bet they're ...'

'That's another thing,' I said. 'I don't allow no liquor, nor no dirty talk in my outfit. You'll find those rules apply on most spreads in Texas.'

'What do you mean?' Hagerty said. 'You ain't *got* a spread.'

'Yeah, but I'm *going* to have,' I told him. 'Soon.'

* * *

My step-brother stood on the porch of the lopsided lean-to we had built, his thumbs hitched in his gunbelt.

'Where you thinking of taking the cows, Charlie?'

'South-west across the Horsehead Trail and up through New Mexico.'

'You lunkhead. You ain't got a chance. That's Comanche country you gotta cross.'

'So I keep gettin' told.'

'You'd be better advised to go back east up the Chisholm Trail. They say the railroad's reached a Kansas town called Abilene.'

'And maybe it ain't. Maybe that's just a rumour. Nope, JW, my mind's made up. I'm goin' west.'

He was a bit grunty with me on account of our falling out, which was basically because I'd had enough of him telling me what to do just because he was a couple of years older than me. 'OK if I take a few of the boys?'

'Sure.' He gave a caustic laugh. 'Take anyone's fool enough to go.'

I turned on horseback to the scruffy band of 'punchers who were leaning against the corral watching us. I

41

would have preferred to have had ex-soldiers, or ex-Rangers, men who were accustomed to four years of hard fighting. But they all packed a six-gun and knew how to use it, so I shouted out, 'I'm taking my herd across the Horsehead Trail. Any of you boys want to come along? Same pay as usual, but a twenty dollar bonus for danger money.'

Three of the men looked at each other and grinned. The word danger was like a red rag to a bull to them. 'OK with you, Mr Steeck?' one called.

'Sure, pick up your pay and go.'

JW and I had been through a lot together, one way or another, and he came across and gave me his hand. 'Hang on to your hair, you ole sonuvagun. We're still pals, still partners, ain't we?'

'Of course,' I smiled. 'It's just that I aim to do things my way from now on.'

'Best of luck,' he shouted, as we went loping away to cut out my share of the herd. I would leave them with the CV brand for the trail. I gave him a wave without turning back. It was best to cut clean, so we added 2,000 to the 500 we already had and headed back to Freedom.

4

Gideon Claypole had set up shop in Freedom with just a wooden soapbox amid half-built houses on dusty Main Street and issued people with deeds for their land. This was shortly after the independent Lone Star State had been received into the Union and folks wanted to make sure they were in legal possession of what land they had grabbed. Claypole prospered and quickly moved into a plank office of his own nailed on to *The Freedom Fighter*, the weekly news sheet. It was believed he had a finger in that and other pies. Anyhow, there his name was painted large on the false front above his office, 'Gideon Claypole, Attorney-at-Law'. Although he was only twenty-five he had already been elected to the town council. So it gave me some satisfaction to park my bellowing herd of 2,500 cows in the long, wide main street, closing up the ends with wagons and roping off any alleyways. Let him have a pile of bullshit on his doorstep. He talked enough!

Of course, the shopkeepers remonstrated. But, as I said to them, if they didn't like that sort of thing why did they come out West in the first place? Mary Ann's father was in the forefront of those who complained vociferously, but such was the racket from the wild longhorns he didn't get heard. I just grinned, waved, and ignored him, and headed my outfit for the saloon. In fact, we didn't even bother getting off our mustangs, just bobbed our heads under the lintel and rode them straight in there through the batwing doors. We peppered the ceiling with revolver shots just to let Sam the saloon-keeper know we'd arrived. For my taste Freedom was getting far too civilized. We had to stick up for our rights!

'OK, boys,' I shouted. 'Settle down.

We'd better send the ponies outside to join the cows 'fore they mess up the place.' My pinto was already enjoying a luxuriant piss as the saloon floozies gathered round us at the bar. 'Drinks is on me tonight. But that don't extend to the services of these young ladies. My fy-an-cee wouldn't approve of that.'

'Where is the li'l honeybush?' Abel Hagerty enquired. 'This I gotta see.'

'She don't come into a house of ill-repute like this,' I said, passing along the bottle of red-eye. 'She'll be busy in the store. I will present my compliments to her shortly.'

'When he's given hisself some Dutch courage,' Slim cackled.

'Yeah, some gals is more frightenin' than Comanches,' Abel laughed, tipping himself a tumblerful.

'Hear tell she's got a face and temper worse than one,' Jesse Wayne hollered, almost choking on his drink.

'All right, boys, a joke's a joke, an' tonight's our last night to let our hair down, I know, but I don't take kindly to you talking about my lady love like that.'

That only made them laugh the more. The whiskey was really getting to their heads. 'Mary Ann's the sweetest-natured, purtiest, loving-tongued . . .' I was saying when there was a loud shriek and I saw her head stuck over the swing doors.

'*Char-leeeee!* You screw-brained bastard. What the heck you doin' with those lousy deadbeats? What are all these durn cows doin' in our street? You tryin' to give my daddy a heart attack?'

'Somebody say she had a face like a horse?' Hagerty chuckled. 'She's got a bray like one, too. Or more like a mule's.'

'I heard that,' Mary Ann shrieked. 'You lookin' to have your ass kicked down the street?'

I went over to the door to try to soothe her down. 'Come on, Mary Ann. I'm only having a few drinks with my boys. I gotta put the cows someplace. There ain't anywhere else they can be corralled. What do you think of them? Ain't I done well?'

'You call them sow-kissers your boys? These mangy critters your herd? What are you, Charlie, some kinda lunatic? You think you gonna make money outa them? You're thinkin' with your nuts. And why you got them gutter trash along? You asking for trouble, or what?'

'Come on, Mary Ann,' I said. 'This is my last night in town. Gimme a kiss.'

'You can kiss them whores in there, but you ain't kissin' me. You can say goodnight to me, Charlie.'

At that point Claypole's fair-curled head suddenly popped up beside hers. 'Why do you associate with this low-life, Mary Ann?'

'You what?' I roared, and reached out to grab him by his necktie, dragging him into the saloon. 'That there's my gal.'

'Unhand me, you smelly villain,'

Claypole protested, trying to wrest my fingers from his tie, as his stud popped and his celluloid collar went awry. Suddenly his bony fist flashed out and collided uncomfortably with my nose, rocking me on my heels and sending me sprawling on the floor. 'Take that,' he said, turning to smile at Mary Ann. 'These types don't like a good punch to the snout.'

'Types?' I had to admit that had made my eyes water. I'd heard the splat as he connected. Wouldn't be surprised if it was broke. I lay and looked at the spurted blood on my hand. 'Villain?' I growled, hanging onto a chair leg to haul myself up. 'I'll teach you villain.'

'Quick, Gideon,' Mary Ann hooted. 'Kick him in the pills, 'fore he gets on his feet.'

'Lousy pen-pushin' lawyer.' Claypole was too slow, or gentlemanly, to take her good advice. He looked like a startled rabbit as my chair crashed across his shoulders and sent him bowling across the floor. The whores whooped as I hauled him to his feet and smacked him a hard right to the jaw that spun him somersaulting, back over a table. 'You keep your paws offen my fy-an-cee while I'm away. Or else.'

Claypole scrambled to his feet somewhat dazed and we began flailing at each other with our fists. 'You cur,' he gasped. 'Mary Ann is my girl.'

That made me see red. And I went for him with a flurry of blows that knocked him down to the floorboards again. Suddenly a saucepan *doinged* off the back of my head. And *doinged* again. 'Ouch!' I yelled, ducking away as Mary Ann rained blows at me with the kitchen implement. 'Whadya doin', gal?'

Pandemonium reigned as other men in the packed saloon leapt into the affray, and me and the boys swung haymakers to defend ourselves, while Mary Ann spun like a wild Dervish laying out with her pan at anyone in her path. The girls jumped in to pull at her hair and try to restrain her.

'Keep away from me you filthy harlots,' she cried, crowning several with the saucepan. Such was her anger we all, men and girls, backed off from her, and simmered down. She stood all-conquering like the ancient Queen of England and glowered at us. 'Keep back you God-useless immoral assholes.' I had to admit her anger was magnificent.

'What's he done to you, Gideon?' Mary Ann knelt down slapping the semi-conscious lawyer's cheeks. 'Speak to me!'

'He started it,' I said. 'Look what he done do by dose. He hid me widdoud warnin'.' I showed her the blood dripping on to my palm.

'Daddy was right. You — you're just an uncouth cowboy.' She helped Gideon up, hauling him over her shoulder. 'You bully. How could you attack this gentleman? Come on, Gideon, let's get out of this haven of Hell. Let them go to the Devil.'

We watched, awed, as she half-carried the boy-lawyer through the batwing doors. 'Whoo!' I whistled. 'What a gal! She sure got a way with her.'

Mary Ann poked her nose back over the doors and hollered, 'Charlee! Unless you pull your socks up our engagement is over.'

Jesus rubbed his jaw and began picking up unbroken chairs. '*Caramba!*' he cried. 'Anybody marry that gal — they welcome to her.'

For moments, I had to admit, I kinda agreed with him as I felt at the bumps on the back of my cranium, and held my head back to try to stop my nose bleeding.

But, the professor of piano had restarted jangling the ivories, the bad gals were screeching like parrots, and the boys were splitting another bottle of Knock-em-Dead, and the evening passed on into rowdy oblivion as I tried to figure out just what Mary Ann was up to.

* * *

At dawn we woke in the sprawled positions on the wooden sidewalk where we had been thrown out of Sam's in the early hours, and groaned as loud as the longhorns looking mournfully down at us. 'Come on, boys,' I said, kicking the other varmints awake. 'We got work to do. Let's get this herd movin'.'

We mounted our mustangs and did so, somewhat hungover, and were yippin' and yellin' herding those dogies out of Freedom when one made a dash for liberty and I had to set my paint galloping back after it through the main drag, slapping my lariat and making it go jumping and bouncing back in the right direction.

'Don't you give nobody no peace?' Mary Ann stuck her head, with funny rags in her hair, out of an upstairs window. 'How are you, Charlie?'

'Aw, it ain't broke,' I said, daintily touching my reddened beak. 'That boy's got a punch on him, though.

Mary Ann, you're gonna have ta make up your mind 'tween him and me.'

'Charlie, you sonuvagun, you know I love you,' she grinned. 'But if you ain't back within three months it's gonna have to be him.'

'Yee-haugh!' I yelled, whirling my hat in the air to her. 'You hang on for me, my darlin'. I'll be back for you.'

And I went dashing off after that ornery longhorn, driving him back to the main herd. When I looked back she was leaning out in her night-dress, rags in her hair, waving like crazy. Smelly and uncouth I might be, but I knew I was the equal of Claypole, and I felt fire in my chest as I waved back. I was ready to risk anything to win that li'l chickadee.

5

The Mexican led us out along the San Saba river to where he had seen all those longhorns roaming loose in the unclaimed lands and we had no trouble in picking up another bunch of 500 to add to our herd. We spent a day or two roping, throwing and branding them, and it was hot, dusty work. We now had a good 3,000 head and only nine men to trail them. I could have done with double that number, so I decided to call it quits, and move the cows up towards the Rio Concho and on to Fort Belknap.

I had been watching Abel Hagerty and his two sidekicks and, although they weren't expert cowhands and were generally laggardly, whining about having to take their turn nightwatch, they would have to do. With his sardonic manner, Hagerty was one of those men who thought himself very superior to ordinary mortals, and liked riling everybody. I soon found out I was not exempt. Before the war I had done a bit of bull-whacking, driving a forty-oxen freight from the frontier post of Fort Worth out to Palo Pinto County. Texas can occasionally get its share of blizzards and in one of these one of my feet froze. Consequently I had walked with a pronounced limp ever since. It meant I never cared to join in any dancing and I guess I was a mite sensitive about it. Hagerty saw this and quickly burrowed deep, making cracks about 'Why don't you get yourself a crutch?' and suchlike. The boys went steely silent on such occasions, but I tried not to show it bothered me. Why should I worry about a mealy-mouthed cuss like him when I was owner of all I surveyed?

* * *

What a fine sight it was from saddle height, a herd of 3,000 healthy, half-wild longhorns forging ahead across purple sage flats, a heaving sea of brute nature, tramping, stamping and bellowing, strong necks, narrow rumps, broad backs and the magnificent tossing horns, surging on like a brown river across the plain. The sun blazed down on us as we rode back and forth, yipping and chivvying them on, but the lead bull did much of our work for us, a big, black stud who had fought other bulls for the honour of being boss, and had got gored for his pains. We had treated his wounds with *tecole* grease to stop the maggots, and he looked proud as punch to lead the way not realizing that our trek would eventually lead to the slaughter yards.

Disease is a big problem for Texan cattle, or anywhere in the hot southlands, with uncountable worms and ticks attempting to eat them alive. We had dosed them as best we could because we didn't want to lose many of the valuable beasts. The sight of a flock of blackbirds swooping down to settle on their backs was a welcome one for they would peck the ticks and bugs from their hides. Thick droves of buzzing horseflies had also joined our march and, although these and other insects were tiresome to the extreme, I felt so cheerful to be on the move I often burst into song — 'Meet me tonight behind the bunkhouse . . . after the cows have settled down' — and other jolly ditties.

A young freed slave, Moses, had joined us at Freedom. I had found him sitting on a barrel outside the saloon, ragged and barefoot, his woolly hair full of dust. He had walked out of a cotton plantation in Louisiana and headed West, but he didn't have much idea of where he was going, or what he was going to do with his freedom. I fitted him out with tough denim jeans, a pair of ex-army boots, and a canvas wind-shedder coat, a ten-dollar Colt .45 and a mustang, similarly priced, and took him along. He was a skinny kid, but the wide grin he gave me whenever he passed, or the way he joined in my singing with deep bass harmony, showed that he'd stick with us to the end.

I was heading the herd towards Fort Belknap mainly because this was a trail I was familiar with, and I knew there were waterholes. We camped the night at one of these and I was pleased to note the herd had settled into an orderly pattern. Of course, nobody knows when cows are likely to panic or stampede at the slightest cause so I set us turns to watch and quieten them through the night.

It was when Abel Hagerty cantered in at midnight from his first four-hour shift that I realized that the herd was not going to be my biggest problem. That would be three of my herders. Moses had rolled himself in a blanket to catch some sleep by the fireside and the one-eyed veteran of Shiloh swung from his mustang and aimed a vicious kick into the pit of his back. 'Git up, you lousy Nigra, this ain't no time to be lazin' before the fire.'

I was over in the dark saddling Paddy, my paint, preparing to take my turn at watch and Abel didn't notice me. Moses yelped with pain, and rolled to his feet, and the fire glowed on the blade of a knife he snatched from the sand.

'Yeah, come on, black boy.' Hagerty's seven-inch barrelled Remington .45 came out from his scabbard fast as lightning and was pointed at Moses' heart as he cocked it with his thumb. 'You want to try me?'

Moses' eyes rolled wildly. His own Colt was tucked under his saddle by the fire and he was no expert with it yet, whereas the speed of Hagerty's draw gave me the impression he was some kind of fast gun. 'Wha' yo' do thet of?' Moses whined. 'I was ready to git up. Yo' ain' no cause to kick me.'

'Wha' yo' do thet fo?' Slim, in his army forage cap, mimicked him, and

Jesse Wayne, who had been out with them tending the herd, giggled.

'Jest look at the tough li'l Nigra. He spoke to a white man like that where ah come from he'd git strung up.'

'Yeah, you watch your mouth, boy, and jump to it,' Hagerty sneered, slowly returning his revolver to its holster. 'It's your turn on watch.'

'Why you no leave the kid alone?' Jesus called out as he, too, roused himself from his blanket back in the rocks. 'Why you keep riding him?'

'Hey, it's the lousy greaser?' Jesse guffawed. 'I thought there was a stink drifting from somewhere.'

The other boys had been disturbed from their slumbers and were beginning to look decidedly edgy.

'Look at li'l Mister Baldicoot,' Slim drawled. 'One of them rats from south of the border. We shoulda run them back across the river years ago when we won the war.'

'Aw, what would be the use?' Jesse laughed. 'They breed like a plague of rabbits. Dirty little runts.'

Jesus sprang to his feet, flicked his purple-striped serape aside to reveal the six-gun in his leather belt. 'You lousy gringos want to shut your mouths.'

'Yeah?' Abel Hagerty faced him, his long, lean fingers hovering over the notched butt of his Remington. 'You gonna make us, son?'

'No, I am,' I said, stepping out of the darkness and jabbing my carbine barrel hard into Hagerty's spine. I reached forward and slipped out his revolver. 'You all three gonna shut your mouths. I don't want no talk like this in my outfit.'

'What are you, a Nigger lover?' Hagerty drawled, his one eye gleaming as he turned to me. 'I might remind you we fought to keep these damn slaves where they belong.'

I cracked him across his jaw with his revolver butt, knocking him down. 'Looks like you lost.'

Hagerty knelt on the sand and spat blood, his face tense with hatred. His *compadres* eyed each other shiftily, but made no move for their guns. If they did, Moses and Jesus were ready for them. 'You'll live to regret that,' Hagerty snarled.

'Maybe. Maybe not. We'll see.' I removed the bullets from the revolver and chucked it back at him. 'I told you when you joined us what I say goes. And I say I don't want you causing trouble with my crew. If you don't like it, you're free to go now.'

Hagerty got to his feet and poured himself a mug of coffee, hot and black. 'So, you're a big man with a damn big mouth?' he grunted. 'What's there to damn well eat?'

'Not beans again?' Jesse groaned.

'You'll eat what you get,' I growled. 'And you'll like it. As I said, you can all go now, but once we hit the trail proper the only way anyone quits is feet first. You got that?'

'Sure, sure,' Hagerty said. 'Why don't you go serenade your damn cows.'

I jerked my head at the other two and we went to climb on our ponies. 'Thanks, boys,' I muttered to them as we rode out, 'for not losing your tempers.'

'My trigger finger was getting mighty itchy,' Jesus said, with a flashing grin. 'Them are three bad gringos.'

'Don't take no notice, Moses,' I said, reaching over to slap his shoulder. 'Some of these southerners didn't like losing the war and they ain't taken kindly to the new order.'

We rode out quietly and crooned lullabies to the cows as we guarded them. It seemed to soothe them. The worst scenario for a cattleman is a stampede. A mosquito bite or a coyote howl could set them off and, apart from those gored and killed in the rush, would leave them looking lank and weary and lacking pounds of valuable fat. I watched the Big Dipper, the saucepan formation of stars in the sky, and when it had completed its full rotation around the North Star and was lined up directly below it I knew it was 4 am. I wanted to move out in the cool hours of the pre-dawn and early morning so I called the boys in and we jogged our ponies back to the camp-fire. The three Arkansas badasses were snoring snugly, so I gave Hagerty a kick in the rump just by way of some of his own medicine.

'Come on,' I roared. 'Let's move 'em out. We ain't got all day to hang about.'

* * *

It's my experience that it don't bode well to be too optimistic, especially on the frontier. So far, in spite of Hagerty's jibes, we had done well. But about high noon that day I saw a sight that veritably chilled my blood.

Up a rise, a great horde of Comanches was moving fast. Their harsh features were decked in feather headdresses and painted for war, as were their lean sun-blackened bodies, their bare legs gripping their fast-moving horses, surging towards us, lances and bows held in their hands, buffalo-skin shields on their arms. And they were uttering that peculiar Comanche scream which once heard can never be forgotten. I swallowed my saliva hard, and looked about. I'd no need to shout a warning. We'd all seen and heard them by now.

'Christ!' Hagerty's jaw dropped as he reached for his Remington and checked it. 'There must be two hundred of them. What we gonna do? We ain't got a chance.'

We were riding point, trying to slow the herd, because the young lead bulls had been vying for position and led the main herd away too fast. In fact, we virtually had two herds, one of about 2,000 head up in front, and another of 1,000 laggards further behind.

'There ain't much we can do,' I yelled, pulling my carbine from the double girth. 'Except try to save the back ones.'

We galloped back pell mell, dashing

across between the two herds, screaming to the men to turn the back herd, and that we managed to do, turning them away in a semi-circle back the way they had come.

'Take cover,' I said, beckoning with my rifle for the boys to join me in the middle of a row of rocks. We leapt from our horses and hunkered down, carbines and revolvers at the ready. I knew I had to sacrifice the front herd and at that moment didn't have a lot of hope of any of us coming out alive.

They hit us like a great tidal wave, hooves pounding, mouths open, screaming the war shriek, arrows ripping the air, their noise drowning the crack and concatenation of our guns as we kneeled to meet them. The ground seemed to throb with their thundering rush. So close, some pitched from their saddles by our lead; so close they were on us; so close they were over us, hooves brushing our heads as we cowered down. One had leaped from his pony, pulling me over, his thin, bangled arm around my throat. I glimpsed a tomahawk raised and fired my carbine into his face. He screamed as it splintered apart in blood and bone. I clambered to my feet and swung the carbine like a club at another who had pranced down lightly in front of me, his knife raised. His head, too, cracked apart and spilled blood. But the first surge had gone and, as I looked around, I saw that we were all still standing, except for Moses who was sprawled on his back with an arrow in his chest.

At first I thought they were going after the smaller herd, but they were turning, re-forming for another charge, screaming their war cry. I tried to keep one eye on them and at the same time concentrate to take bullets from my belt and feed them into the carbine magazine. Done. I snapped it shut and knelt to take aim again.

We had already brought a good many down and they were lying prostrate. One Comanche was writhing and thrashing in madness, torn by his broken spine. And painted ponies, too, some struggling to rise, broken and bleeding. 'Reload your revolvers,' I shouted. 'Let them get close. Choose your man and fire.'

It was easier said than done, faced by yet another massive cavalry charge, a mighty surge of thrashing pony hooves, howling throats, heads crested by eagle feathers. And razor-sharp steel slashed at us as they leapt. They had to leap. Our bulwark of rocks saved us. Mechanically I levered my carbine, heard the explosions, saw an agony of shattered bone, saw an oiled-brown body coming down on me, knocking my breath from me, grappling to hold me. The savage face so close, suddenly collapsed upon me. As I rolled him away, I saw the Mexican's gun smoking and he flashed me a grin as the Comanche horde galloped on. How a man can grin at such a time I do not know. Some enjoy the fight.

'Reload,' I shouted again, and noted that Hagerty, too, was pretty cool, standing with his long-barrelled revolver outstretched aimed at their backs as they thundered away.

It seemed the fire power of our repeating carbines and revolvers had surprised them, as it had that time with the Rangers on the Pirandelles. They were regrouping again, but, instead of another charge, sent a shower of arrows our way. We ducked our heads behind our nest of rocks, and one of the 'punchers was hit, sobbing with agony. We quickly knelt to return a volley of shots, blasting several more into Eternity.

I glanced around and guessed we had cut down at least forty of them. They would not like that. And this showed, when instead of a frontal assault they broke and began circling around at a ragged lope, hanging on the far side of their mustangs, so we could not get a good aim, firing their arrows under the horses' necks, superb horsemen. The panthers of the plains, some call them.

If they had wanted, I guess, they could have worn us down. There were only seven of us left. Our ammunition would not last for ever. But nor would their arrows. Some of the chiefs, in their big, flowing headdresses, were having a discussion. They raised their lances, hurled insults at us, and turned away. Hadn't they stolen our vast herd of cattle? Their pride was assuaged. Other warriors screamed and yipped and trotted away on their ponies, not deigning to look back, or bother about their dead.

'Jeez,' I whispered. 'I believe they've had enough.'

We stood close to each other, our bodies redolent of sweat, the sweat of fear. Hagerty cursed, strode over to one fallen brave, picked up a tomahawk and hacked off his scalp. He brandished it and grinned. 'His spirit will be roaming bald in the afterworld.' His mates, Slim and Jesse, joined him in taking trophies while we others looked on dazedly.

'That's enough!' I shouted. 'We're

not savages.' Surely they deserved some dignity in death, although they would have given us none. 'Let's put the injured out their misery before Hagerty decides to have fun with 'em.'

'*Nombre de Dios*!' Jesus called. 'Look! This one he is a Mexican.'

'Yeah.' Hagerty scowled at him. 'I saw others of you filthy greasers among them.'

'*Comancheros*,' I said. 'They work hand in glove. It ain't nothing to do with Jesus so leave him out of it.'

'Yeah!' Jesus laughed, hysterically. 'I no know heem. He too ugly for my family. But what is this? *Caramba*!' He fished pieces of silver from the dead man's pocket. 'Just what I need.'

I put my revolver to the head of dying horses and Comanches and helped them on their way. I went to take a look down the hill but the raiding party had gone, and my main herd, too. All that I could see was a distant amber dustcloud moving away into a crimson backwash as the sun fell

72

into the vast barren country.

'Moses is in a bad way,' Jesus said when I returned. 'Tom Stone's dead.'

Tom lay with an arrow through his throat. I took a wallet from his jacket. 'I'll send it to his family,' I said.

Moses had foolishly broken off the haft of the arrow in his upper chest and the flint was embedded deep. His face was blue-grey and dust-runnelled with tears he could not control. 'I'm gonna die, boss,' he gasped.

'No you ain't. Hang on in.' I went and caught Paddy, who had skittered away from the shooting, but was peaceably nibbling at a thorn bush. I took a pair of horseshoe pliers from my saddle-bag, and went back to Moses. I slipped my knife between his teeth. 'Bite on that. Someone hold him down.' I got a grip on the arrow-head and jerked it out. I broke open a bullet casing, sprinkled powder on the wound, lit a match, set it alight. He screamed. 'That should cauterize it. He'll be all right, as long as the head ain't pizened. Help him on his hoss. It's no use hanging around here. We gotta go find those other cows.'

We caught up with the rear herd, who hadn't, luckily, stampeded, but just slowed their pace. A rough count showed me there was about 1,000 head. I took a deep breath and looked back towards where the Comanches had disappeared. It seemed to me they were heading for the Horsehead Trail, too.

'Well, a thousand's better than nothing.' I gave a rueful grin. 'When JW hears about this he's gonna laugh his damn socks off. That's my share gone.'

It broke the tension. They eased their rank-smelling bodies on their broncs and grinned at me, wiped their brows with bandannas. 'You boys will be glad you've got some hair left to comb. You ready to push on overnight towards the fort? I don't fancy hanging around here tonight.'

'Sure.' Hagerty tied the bloody scalp to his saddle horn. 'Let's vamoose.'

6

The herd was going at a good clip and they went even faster when they smelt water as the stream and stockade of Fort Belknap hove into view. 'Hold on!' I cried, as I peered through the clouds of dust from my position at the rear. 'There's another herd already there.' I sent Paddy galloping forward shouting to the three ex-soldiers riding point, 'Haul 'em in, you idiots. Slow 'em down. Turn them away.'

But it was too late. The herd was intent on reaching water and no amount of cursing and whip cracking was going to stop them. They just trotted on, bellowing and boneheaded and ran right into the other herd, merging into each other like water.

The boss of the other herd came flying up at me on his big chestnut stallion. He was as angry as I was. 'What the hell you doing?' he hollered. 'Ain't you got any sense?'

'It's them lunkheads riding point,' I shouted. 'They been busy killin' blue-bellies. They ain't used to cows. But, I guess I'm to blame. I got to apologize to you, mister.'

He was a broad-chested man, in his fifties, wearing a dusty city suit and blue-spotted bandanna. His face was tanned and lined like old leather, humour lines around the eyes which gleamed bright blue, and when he pushed his tall hat back with a forefinger it showed hair of grizzled grey.

'What's done is done,' he growled. 'But it's gonna take the best of four days to cut them cows apart and sort 'em out.'

We watched my bulls already battling for supremacy with his bulls and I tossed him a pouch of Bull Durham to roll a cigarette. 'Do ya mind if we do that tomorrow? My men are just about done in. We had a set-to with the Comanche.'

'So I see,' he said, as he lit up, and eyed Tom Stone's body tied over a horse. 'How many of 'em?'

'A war party of two hundred. There's about a hundred and sixty now.'

He gave a whistle of awe, and nodded at Moses, who was hanging onto the neck of his mustang. 'What happened to him?'

'Arrow in his chest. He should pull through. They got a surgeon here?'

'Yes, I'll take you in. My boys will look after the beeves. Don't worry.' As we rode in, leading Moses, the herd boss glanced at me. 'You look pretty sick for a man who's escaped death.'

'They got the bulk of my herd, two thousand head.'

He whistled again. 'That's a lot of valuable beeves to lose. Where the hell were you going?'

'Fort Sumner.'

He savoured this as we ambled into the fort, pulled in our horses, and I

77

helped Moses down, sat him in the shade.

'My name's Loving. Oliver Loving. I'll take you to meet the captain.'

'I'm Charlie Goodnight.'

Loving? That name had a familiar ring. Most men had heard of him. An old frontiersman of considerable repute, who in '55 had driven a herd as far as Illinois.

'Where you planning on taking yours?' I asked.

'I had hoped to get to Denver. I'd get a good price at the mining camps. But there's no way we could make it across The Staked Plains. The Comanche would gobble us up, horses, cattle and men.'

'You're not kidding.'

Captain Arthur Hennessy was a spruced-up Yankee dude, but affable enough. I reported the attack and Tom Stone's death.

'He was a big-chinned, fair-haired, easy-going fellow,' I told him. 'I'd known him for years.'

'In that case he must have known the odds on staying alive aren't good in these unholy parts,' Hennessy snapped. 'Where on earth were you heading? Don't you people realize this is a war zone?'

'Aren't you going after them?'

'That's my business.'

'We're taking the Horsehead Trail. I want to get my cattle through to New Mexico.'

'That's madness.' He was writing down Tom's details in his log. 'Isn't one man dead enough? You'll never get through.'

'So everybody says. Any chance of a military escort?'

'No chance. We have other things to do than worry about a few crazy Texan cowboys. You think we're going to trail along with you?'

I got up to my feet, wearily. 'I got another wounded man needs medical attention. He's black.'

'Black or white, he'll get the same treatment. Take him to the dispensary.'

Oliver Loving followed me out. 'You know that Horsehead Trail is nigh on a hundred miles without a drop of water? You'll find nothing wetter than sunbaked mud. You might lose more cows than you get through. There's a chance you might meet more Comanches.'

'I'll take that chance.'

He grabbed hold of my arm and faced me. 'If you let me come, I'll go with you.'

'Well,' I smiled. 'It would save having to cut out our cows.'

'Partners? My thousand head and yours? Equal share.'

'Partners.' I shook his hand again. 'I tell you, Mr Loving, this is a feasible cattle trail. Agreed, it's never been done, but there's allus a first time.'

He pointed to a map pinned to the wall outside the guard post. 'You see that? Follow the Pecos up to Fort Sumner. It's one straight line north through Pueblo, and then Denver, right up to Cheyenne, mainly avoiding

Comanche country. I think we're on to something, Charlie.'

'Hell right we are.'

* * *

Moses was groggy, but the surgeon put him on a cot, said I'd done a good job, all he needed was rest.

'Don't leave me here, Mr Goodnight,' Moses murmured, before he passed out.

'We'll need a couple of days to stock up on supplies. But, if he ain't ready by then we'll have to go.'

'Of course. That's the way the cookie crumbles. You know, Charlie, I can't wait to get started on the Loving-Goodnight Trail.'

'Goodnight-Loving sounds better,' I said.

* * *

An inventor was not something I ever planned on being. But it is generally agreed that I invented the mainstay and centre-bit, the focal point of every round-up throughout the West — the good old chuck wagon. It happened at Fort Belknap as Oliver and I were splitting a bottle of whiskey with Captain Hennessy. We were working out how much we needed to buy, how many sacks of flour, sugar, salt, dried fruit, onions, potatoes, green coffee beans and pinto beans for the trek. On top of that we would need to carry heavy equipment like rifles, branding irons, horseshoes, axe and shovel, pots and skillets, a Dutch oven, pot hooks, kerosene, axle grease, water canteens, not to mention the giant coffee pot.

'We're gonna need a whole team of mules to carry this stuff,' Oliver Loving said, making a wry face as he supped the whiskey.

Most of the time a cowhand would carry all he needed on horseback, his bedroll and lariat, slicker and rifle stuck through the cinch of the saddle. But the latter would snag the reins and weigh him down badly when cutting out cows. On a long trail his packhorse would be a necessity. I began to wonder if this extra gear couldn't be transported more easily and, as I did so, I glanced out of the door at a solid four-wheeled army wagon with its extra-durable iron axles. 'You ain't got one of them wagons for sale, have you, Commander?' I said to Captain Hennessey, almost jokingly. 'We could put all our equipment on that.'

'We do have some surplus to our needs now the war's over,' he replied, refilling our glasses. 'I'd be glad to sell one at cost price.'

So, that's how it began. Over the next couple of days that followed, as Oliver busied himself spraying the cattle with kerosene, a cure-all, he figured, against bugs and ticks, and buying and shoeing about sixty good horses for our remuda, I set to figuring out the most compact design for our wagon.

We were lucky that the fort's sutler

had been so well supplied for we could buy most everything we needed, including an extra wagon wheel, which I placed inside the bed of the wagon along with the bedrolls, ammunition, rifles and a big can of axle grease, all with easy access. On the side of the wagon I built a platform to hold a barrel with water for two or three days' supply for the men. On the other side I put a big tool box, not forgetting a shovel. We might need to do some burying.

Now I scratched my noddle wondering where to stash the rest of the smaller stuff. As I did so, two soldiers carried out from the captain's office one of those high wooden chests honeycombed with drawers and cubby holes for storing files and suchlike. They pitched it onto the dust. It had been made by a master craftsman, but was a trifle scratched so no doubt not up to the captain's specifications. 'Don't you want this?' I asked.

'No,' one said. 'It's for firewood.'

'Maybe we could use it. Would you boys mind just lifting it up and seeing if it will fit across the back of the wagon? There we go. That's right.' With the drawers facing outwards it was a perfect fit. 'Sure you don't want it?'

'It's yours. Saves us the job of chopping it up. What you gonna do with it?'

'See all these drawers? They're perfect for keeping everything handy — molasses, baking soda, salt, coffee beans, bandages, chewing and rolling baccy, string, needles and thread, stewing beans, sugar, matches, pot hooks, even medicinal whiskey and castor oil, all handy for the cook.'

When they had gone I fixed it secure, bought a pot of gold paint and amused myself putting the names of all the different items on the various drawers. The big drawer at the bottom I kept for pots and pans. The wagon flap could be raised when on the move and lowered for use as a table.

I rigged up a canvas bag below the

wagon so as we went along we could toss in any good bits of dry wood for the fire. And, as a final flourish, fixed a coffee grinder protruding from one side. On the tail board I hung a hurricane lamp. And I made bentwood bows for a canvas covering as protection against sun and rain. *Voila*! as them Frenchies say. The chuck wagon was born.

When I drove the completed article out yoked to ten pairs of oxen, the men gathered around slapping me on the back and cheering as I explained what it was all about. 'You surprise me, Charlie,' Loving said. 'You really do. It's a work of inspiration. You ought to patent it.'

Years later, I wished I had because the famous Studebaker Company brought out an identical chuck wagon selling for $100.

Only Abel Hagerty seemed un-impressed. He gave a twisted sneer and muttered that we were all like a lot of kids.

Loving had ten men, most of whom

seemed honest enough, some the usual scruffy 'puncher who you would find hanging around any fort or township on the lam, the others tough ex-Confederates, looking to earn a few dollars and ready for any adventure.

'I ain't too keen on them three soldier boys of yours,' he said to me, as we sat around the campfire the night before we moved out.

'They were at Shiloh so they musta got some guts. They're just a bit sour, thassal. They fought well against the Comanch'.'

'Don't know about Shiloh. I heard a rumour they rode with William Quantrill and Bloody Bill Anderson under the Black Flag, with Jesse James and his cousin, Cole Younger. The devils claimed to be fighting for the south, but they slaughtered civilians to line their own pockets. A band of two hundred murderous cut-throats, that's all they were. And since the war some of 'em have drifted south.'

'What shall I do? I've hired 'em now.'

'There ain't nobody else to be had so I guess we better keep 'em. We need eighteen men for this job. But I don't like it, I can tell you that.'

★ ★ ★

'Hell, I'm not leaving Moses,' I told Jesus, and we loaded him into the chuck wagon to take it easy until he was able to ride.

'Let's move,' I shouted, and we rolled out of the fort gates and got the herd moving following the old Butterfield Stage line that, before the war, had gone at a cracking pace across western Texas, through New Mexico and Arizona to Los Angeles fearless of Comanches, Apaches or white robbers. We went at a much slower pace, 250 miles ahead of us before we reached the headwaters of Rio Concho and our troubles began. The only trouble we had had at the fort was a heifer who, sprayed

88

with disinfecting kerosene, wandered through a branding fire and turned into a cattle torch. Waste not want not. We cut out the best meat from the poor critter, sliced it thin, and dried it in the broiling sun to keep it for the trail.

At first all went well; as always, with a fresh start, the cowboys in high spirits, yodelling and hollering as they drove our double herd along. Even the horn-clickering longhorns seemed in a good mood, settling down to a good pace.

Loving had appointed a lanky, bald-headed galoot as cook in charge of the chuck wagon. Known as Sonuvabitch Stevens, on account of his sullen nature, nearing sunset we would send him forward to find a spot to camp, and, as we trailed in, he would have a welcoming fire lit, and the coffee hot. His last job at night was to point the wagon tongue to the north star, so we had a makeshift compass to guide us at dawn.

On the second day, one of the cows decided to calf. The calf wasn't strong enough to make the trek, and it just shows what a cheerful, sentimental bunch we must have been to start with because we decided to carry him. I took first turn to have him straddled across Paddy's neck in front of my saddle, and pretty soon cowboys were riding up almost begging me to let them take their turn with the li'l critter. His mother trotted along nearby, contentedly.

I guess us cowpokes are a simple bunch because as we sat around the campfire eating our supper there was much guffawing at practical jokes like tying a man's spurs together when he hadn't noticed and watching him take a dive in the dust. Or hiding a rattler in his bedroll!

And the boys vied to boast about the hardships of their particular neck of the woods. A youngster named Trinity Tom said the wind was so strong up on the plains in Colorado it would blow a guard dog on a chain out at right angles to the ground. A slow-drawling Texan, funnily enough known as Tex, told us his whole farm had been picked up and set down twenty miles away by a tornado and he was asleep all the time.

We had hired a wrangler, Jim Drum, to look after the remuda of mustangs, which was roped off at night. When asked if he had ever been thrown from a horse, 'Nope,' was his nonchalant reply. 'Where I come from when a hoss sets in bucking we jest sit there and roll a cigareet. So it seems it's useless to try.'

'That's nothing,' a wag called Willy Henry had to put in. 'In Clay County we break 'em in while we're taking a shave.'

This was all good-humoured stuff, but these were early days. The trail crew weren't going to be so cheerful in days to come. Needless to say, the only three who didn't join in the fun were the three saddlebum soldiers from

Arkansas, but maybe they didn't get the jokes. Folks up there are renowned for being a trifle dense. Or maybe they didn't want to.

The only tale I heard Abel Hagerty tell was how in the war he would truss prisoners back to back and shoot them both with one bullet to save ammunition. A cheerful soul! He was forever fiddling with his Remington revolver, a fine, slim, state-of-the-art weapon, recently converted from cap and ball to take the new brass cartridges. He was continually squinting with his one eye along the sights of the solid frame on its top which gave it added strength, or be whipping it from his holster and spinning it on a finger to show how fast he was.

'Frank James uses one of these,' he crowed. 'He once tol' me it's the hardest and surest shooting pistol ever made.' The boys looked askance at each other and fell quiet for none wished to try to prove otherwise.

Nor did his sidekick, Jesse Wayne,

get a laugh when he called over to him, 'You remember when we sent them Kansas redlegs on foot through that minefield ahead of us? The way they got blowed to bits on their own bombs? That sure was funny.'

I don't know about funny. Them three fellers just made us feel a mite uncomfortable.

7

All the indications were that the Year of Our Lord 1866 would go down as the year of the great drought in the American West. And so it proved. The month of June and not a cloud in the great blue arc of sky. A desert land of parched plateau stretched out before us where even the cactus and scrub barely managed to retain enough water to survive. All the streams and waterholes were low and the rains had failed to come. We urged our 2,000 head across this barren waste, but we knew this was the easy part. The worst was yet to come.

Moses had insisted on getting on his feet. Maybe horseback was easier to bear than the hard rutting of the wagon. I was easy on him, letting him ride flank rather than drag where he would have to be masked to the eyes by his neckerchief eating the herd's stifling dust cloud. Of course Hagerty had to make jibes about favouritism. In spite of the pain I knew he was suffering, Moses' black face broke into a grin whenever we passed. He was a good kid.

We had taken to putting our pet calf in the chuck wagon, but whether other cows had an idea their offspring would be similarly treated or not, I don't know, but they started dropping calves with frequent regularity. Cows find it difficult to keep up with adult steers, and calves have no chance. We piled a few more in the wagon, but it was a foolish enterprise. In the end I was compelled to slaughter them, apart from our first one. It was something I hated doing, and I made up my mind never to trail a mixed herd again across such a hard route.

On we went along the Middle Concho forty miles to its head-waters. There we let the cattle rest, let them fill their skins with water in preparation

95

for the terrible test to come. And then it was, 'Onwards, ho!' The dreaded ninety-six mile dry leg of the drive had begun.

All day the herd tramped across the high chapparal, a great cloud of bitter alkali dust rising from them. When you rode close you could feel the intense heat of their bodies, like an oven blast. The second day they began to get very restless with thirst, and their tongues began to loll, as they bemoaned their fate, their eyes rolling.

'It's worse than I thought,' Oliver Loving muttered to me. 'Hot and dead as hell. No sign of water, not even a damned puddle.'

'All we can do is keep 'em going,' I gritted out. 'If they stop and lie down they'll never rise again.'

It was as if the cattle knew this, for the second night they did not rest. Desperate with thirst they milled and trampled about through the dark hours so I had to call everybody in the outfit out to hold them.

'This will never do,' I said the next morning, as we drank bitter black coffee. 'These cattle walked around enough last night to have got to the Pecos. We won't stop tonight. We've got to let them travel.'

'Guess you're right, Charlie,' Loving said. 'You take charge. See what you can do.'

But it wasn't as easy as that. As the sun rose high and its heat beat down on us, the stronger cattle forged ahead and the weaker ones lagged behind until keeping the herd together became a worrying problem.

I rode back and forth on my blocky paint, Paddy, now at point, now at the flank, directing and encouraging, getting the point riders to hold the leaders back so the front and rear would not be too far separated.

'I'll take charge of the drag, Charlie,' Loving volunteered. 'I'll try to save as many laggards as possible.'

'I'll tie an ox-bell to one of the point riders' horses. Whenever you can't hear it send forward and we'll try to hold the leaders.'

The men fell silent as we trudged along, their throats too dry to do any yelling. The only sound was the creak of saddle leather, the jingle of spurs and harness, the forlorn bellowing of the animals. We were strictly rationing the men to drinking water, and had forbidden any luxuries like shaving. That was when I first grew me a beard and I've never had it off since. What's the use of all that business with cut-throat razor, brush, soap and bay rum? you ain't likely to meet any women out in the wilds!

Soon we lost our first cow. She just crumpled to her knees and gave up the ghost, panting and gasping, outstretched on the sand. We didn't have time or inclination to even stop and cut away her hide or good meat. We just kept plodding onwards towards the lowering sun. She was the first of many. Soon the sight of an exhausted longhorn tottering away from the bunch to lie down and die became one of frightening frequency. And I saw the inevitable cloud of turkey vultures up above beginning to circle.

'How many more are we going to lose in God's name?' I asked Oliver Loving as the figures pencilled in my notebook reached 100, then 200, and finally 300 carcasses left to litter the trail. 'We won't have a dang herd left at this rate.'

'It can't be far off now,' Loving croaked out, as he wiped the dust and salt sweat from his face, for the temperature was well up in the 120 mark on the Professor Fahrenheit scale. 'To tell the truth I'm beginning to wonder if we haven't made a big mistake.'

'Aw, nothing ventured, nothing gained, as the maxim goes,' I muttered. 'But I cain't say I'm so happy, either. I was hoping to get married on the proceeds of this trip!'

The cattle were a pitiable spectacle. Their ribs stood out like basketwork, their flanks sagged gauntly, their tongues lolled and heads hung low. Their bellowing had been reduced to pitiable moaning as, half-crazed with thirst, they plodded on. The men weren't in a lot better condition because, as the vast globe of sun began to melt away before us, we discovered our water barrel was dry. Not even a drop for our poor horses. There would be no coffee for the men that night.

'What's happening, Mr Goodnight?' Moses called as we went on into the red haze dust of dusk. 'Ain't we stopping?'

'We just gotta keep on pushing, Moses.' I was sucking on a pebble to try to keep my saliva going. 'Keep on pushing through the night. This stretch of trail cain't go on without end. Though it might seem so right now.'

Some of the men were so worn down from the long hours in the saddle without sleep that they rubbed tobacco into their eyes to keep themselves awake as we went on through the long, dark night. None wanted to be left behind with those sprawled beasts who would be nothing but a pile of bleached bones once the turkey vultures had done with them. There was no joshing now. They just sat staring apathetically ahead, occasionally cracking their lariats to urge the critters on.

Water. That was the one substance on men's minds. And the animals', too. And, as dawn streaked the sky on the morning of that fourth day, as they tottered out through Castle Gap on weak legs, they were greeted by the blessing of a cool breeze. The cattle scented water and went lurching ahead. And, as we stood in our stirrups, the Pecos River could be seen twelve miles away down the decline.

'Great Jehosophat!' I yelled. 'We've done it, Oliver. Damn your lights, you ole cow-sucker, we've done it. We've blazed a trail to go down in history.'

'Not so much of your shouting, Charlie,' Loving said, as what spirit was left in the remainder of our 2,000 beeves began to stir, to moan, to send them breaking into a quickening trot. Suddenly, before we could stop them, they were going at a run towards the river. 'We ain't through yet. We got a stampede on our hands!'

'My God!' I yelled, as we both went speeding to the point. 'Slow them! Turn them!'

But, it was too late, and as I galloped alongside, I knew it. There was a wild running river of hide, horn and hooves, a torrent of terrified animals who were of one mind, to get to water. Out of the corner of my eye I saw Jesus come prancing alongside of me, and then he was gone, swept away on the tide. His cinch must have been broken by a bull's horn for I saw his pony gallop free saddleless in front of me. I looked across and there the little Mexican was crouched on the back of a plunging steer, hanging to his great horns for dear life. I saw a flash of terror in his eyes, and I knew there was only one thing to do: ride into the tumultuous stampede of sabre-sharp horns.

I heeled Paddy over, forced him through, and suddenly I was surrounded by wild-eyed steers, vicious horns flying all about me, any second in danger of being gored, or my horse brought down. Indeed, one of the beeves had been gored or tripped by one of its own and crashed to the ground before us, to be churned by thousands of hooves into an unrecognizable mess. By sheer agility and horse sense, Paddy swerved around the fallen beast while others toppled on top of it, and he seemed to sense what I wanted him to do for we were going full pelt but moving in closer and closer to Jesus. We came up alongside and I screamed out at him to 'Grab hold!' He looked around, saw me, and leaped out to swing onto me behind my saddle, and I urged Paddy out. Gradually we neared the edge and were safe, but I saw a new catastrophe up ahead.

There lay the River Pecos shimmering in the dawn light, a wondrous sight, but, as the longhorns in front tried to stop to drink, the vast rush and weight of beeves behind them pushed them on and on across and right over to the other bank. It was a scene of pandemonium as more steers came crashing down the bank. All I could do was sit and watch as cows, and calves and steers were trampled and drowned, or worse death of all, bogged down in quicksand.

'Whoo! Señor Goodnight,' Jesus whimpered as he hung on behind me. 'Did you ever see such a sight?'

'No,' I said. 'And I don't want to again.'

8

The worst of the journey was over, or so we thought. We had made it through the parched lands. As the sun came up we rode back to count the mangled remains of those beeves crushed or gored in the rush, and added them to those drowned or lost in the quicksands. To the 300 dead from lack of water, we had another 100 lost by their urge for it. We harried them all across Horsehead Crossing and I could see men and beasts were exhausted, so I yelled, 'We'll take a day or two out to rest. Let'em drink their fill and graze. They ain't gonna run nowhere now. You boys can take your ease. That OK with you, Mr Loving?'

'Sure, Charlie,' he said, brushing the dust from his worsted suit, which by now was somewhat ragged. 'We could all do with time out.'

The little calf, our symbol of survival, had been travelling on the chuck wagon so was safe, and suddenly his mother came wandering up searching for him. I handed him down to her and it was a touching sight to see him run to her, and the great licking, mooing and lowing that went on at the reunion. The little calf went at her udder and she was almost beside herself with joy. I'd like to report that I kept that li'l critter as a pet for the rest of his life, but I guess somewhere along the line he got served up on somebody's plate like all the rest. That was their fate, alas.

The sun rose higher and the men dipped in the river, and I even chanced a bathe myself, though keeping my long johns on, and my Spencer close at hand. A man can never be too careful. We were about to enter the land of the Mescaleros.

Stevens cooked up what he called his special Sonuvabitch Stew, using one of the young drowned steers. Lean beef, liver, heart, testicles, brains, marrow, gut, all got chopped up and chucked in the pot and put in his Dutch oven, with a jar of Louisiana hot sauce, salt and pepper. He simmered it for three hours and finally clanged on a frying pan, yelling, 'Come and git it, you deadbeats.' Every man stuffed himself silly, then sat around all afternoon playing craps, or cards, or mending tack, washing shirts, sewing holes, or darning socks.

Abel Hagerty, with his eye patch, and his long greasy hair hanging back to his shoulders, went so far as to take off his tattered Confederate frock coat, and sat on a rock cleaning his Remington. I saw him give a mocking grin and make some remark to his mates as if he found this domestic bliss kinda amusing. I guess that he had witnessed so much killing the past four years it had blunted any tender emotions he once might have had. He didn't understand that to these wandering cowhands being part of a bunch like this was the closest they ever came to being part of a family.

'How about we go take a scout up-river?' Oliver Loving suggested mid-afternoon, and I readily agreed, slinging a saddle on Paddy and cantering away beside his big stallion.

'The Mescaleros are one Apache tribe that's supposed to have been pacified,' I said, 'but you never can tell.'

It wasn't 'Messys' we had to worry about that day. We maybe stayed out too long nosing along the bank of the deep-flowing river, and sat for a while on its bank, having a smoke and a chat, watching its shimmering whorls. It was well past sundown when we got back, and the boys had built up the campfire and seemed to be having a fine old time. Some of them had partnered off and were doing the Texas two-step around the blaze as Trinity Tom scraped on his battered fiddle.

The first thing my nostrils scented was whiskey. It looked to me like Stevens had broken out the flagon kept for medicinal purposes. No doubt they had offered him a few dollars' incentive. 'What in hell's going on?' I hollered as I rode in, and, as they saw me, the whooping and screaming gradually ceased.

'Aw, they wanted to party, Mr Goodnight,' the cook whined. 'I couldn't refuse them.'

I stepped down, and swung round, landing him a pile-driver to the jaw that sent him staggering back to collapse among his pots and pans. 'You stupid sonuvabitch,' I snarled. 'They sure named you right.' I picked up the empty flagon. 'What we gonna use as anaesthetic anybody gits shot?'

'Heck!' Tex laughed, staggering drunkenly towards me. 'What you worryin' fer? We can sit on his head.'

My right came up as I looked at him, but what was the use? A man's love of whiskey outrides his sense. I tossed the flagon away. 'Who's watching the herd?'

'Them three soldier boys. You said

yourself the cows ain't likely to stray,' Tom muttered sulkily, putting his fiddle away.

'Right,' I told them, filling two mugs with coffee for me and Loving. 'You all just simmer down. This is a cattle trail, not some damn picnic.'

'Where's the remuda staked out?' Oliver asked.

'Over in the trees down-river,' Jesus piped up, looking abashed for he'd been joining in the dancing. 'Jim Drum he reckon they be safer there.'

We sat around awhile having some stew and discussing what we'd seen up-river, and it must have been getting on for midnight when I said, 'We'd better go relieve Hagerty.'

'Where's Jim gotten to?'

'He generally sleeps out near the broncs,' Jesus said, as he swung onto his horse to accompany us.

Suddenly the hair prickled on the back of my neck as we ambled our horses through the darkness past the contentedly grazing cows. Where in hell were the guards? What in tarnation was wrong with me? I should sooner have trusted a rattlesnake than Hagerty.

'Where's the remuda?' Loving called.

'It was somewhere round here,' Jesus replied, peering into the trees. There was only a sliver of moon and little light to see by. 'Maybe Jim move them.'

'Maybe Jim didn't,' I said, as Paddy shied away from something, or somebody, lying in the grass. 'Maybe somebody else did. Maybe Jim Drum ain't gonna be moving no more.'

I jumped down, struck a match, and saw his rictus grin of death, the slit across his throat, the matted blood on his shirt. 'This is one good wrangler we've lost.'

'He's dead?' Loving asked, in a strangulated voice.

'As a doorpost. It looks like they've lit out with our remuda.'

'All the horses? Gone?'

'All sixty of 'em. Good stock. While we were taking a gentle ride, them bastards whipped them behind our backs. They must have got a four-hour start.'

'Damnation!' Loving whispered — he didn't often curse — 'Damn their souls. What fools we are!'

'I can't say you didn't warn me. I'm the durn fool for keeping 'em on. How many hosses we got left?'

'There's two hitched by the wagon for the relief guards, and one being shoed,' Jesus said. 'These we're on.'

'Shee-it! Well, there's only one thing to do. Go after 'em.'

'It's pitch dark,' Loving put in. 'We'll have to wait until morning. We won't be able to see any trail.'

'I ain't waiting for no one,' I said. 'They ain't gone north. And they sure as hell ain't gone back into the desert. So they'll be following the river south. Maybe with the dawn they'll branch off, and head west towards the pass through the Sacramento and David Mountains to Mexico. Every second counts if we're gonna catch up with 'em 'fore they reach the border.'

'That figures, *hombre*,' Jesus agreed. 'I come with you.'

'It strikes me that Hagerty was planning all along to head for Mexico an' offer himself and them other two as soldiers of fortune to that Austrian emperor who's fighting to stay on the throne.'

'He is the puppet of the French,' Jesus cried. 'Our true president is Benito Juarez.'

'That's as maybe. But that's where they've as likely gone. And they'll try to sell our hosses on the way.'

'We'll get those other horses,' Oliver said. 'And move out.'

'Nope. I think you ought to stay here, Mr Loving. Somebody responsible's got to guard the herd.'

'In that case, take my stallion, Charlie.'

'Nope. You'll be needing him to ride for help, just in case I don't manage to git back. Paddy'll see me through.'

There was a general palaver back at

the campfire when I told the boys what had happened. 'Who's coming with me? There could be gunplay. Break out the carbines, Stevens. Fifty rounds each. Hard rations each man for four days.'

Moses stepped forwards. 'Take me, boss.'

'Out the way,' Tex said, pushing him aside. 'They need a man who knows how to handle a gun.'

'OK,' I said, as the men clamoured forward. 'Tex, Trinity Tom, and — '

'I got a grudge to settle with that Hagerty,' Moses called. 'I won't let you down, Mr Goodnight.'

'OK, Moses. Get them three mustangs saddled. Hurry. We've got a hard ride.'

★ ★ ★

We were only able to ride at a careful canter over the unfamiliar terrain alongside the river because of the heavy darkness, but we pushed on through the night until dawn began to flush the eastern sky like a peach-coloured lantern. 'Spread out, boys,' I shouted. 'And keep your eyes peeled for spoor.' But there was nothing, no sign of life, except where a herd of antelope had gone down to drink. I began to have doubts and to wish I had waited until daylight to look for their prints. Maybe they had cast off way back. If so, they were lost to us in this vast barely explored region.

It was about 10 am when Moses gave a shout, 'Hey, boss! Here they are.'

'Here they were, you mean,' I said, as I skittered Paddy across. The ground was churned up with hoof-prints and droppings, and there was a pile of ashes. 'That's them for sure. Looks like they took a rest.'

I jumped down and studied the droppings close up. They were cold set. Not recent. I looked at one of the horseshoe marks. Its indentations had a small bird's claw marks imprinted on it. Probably come down to peck at their crumbs. The ash of their fire was faintly warm. 'I'd say they were here three, four hours ago.'

'Is that good?' Moses asked. 'Or bad?'

'A bit of both.' I stirred the ash with a stick, and blew on it to get a glow, tossing on some half-burned remnants of wood. 'Let's have a quick cup of coffee and get on their trail.'

'They've got the hosses to drove,' Tex drawled. 'That's gonna slow 'em down a piece.'

'Yep. And if they stop for breakfast they cain't be in so much of a hurry. Maybe they ain't expecting us to follow.'

'If they ain't they made a bad judgement of us Texans,' I said, as I crushed coffee beans with my carbine butt on a stone.

'And us Coloradoans,' Trinity Tom called as he went to fill the pot with water.

'And us Mexicans,' Jesus grinned.

'And us Louisianans,' Moses added.

'Yeah, I get the picture,' I muttered.

116

It was easy after that to follow the herd's marks as they left the river and headed across the plain. So we rode hard and soon the distant border mountains began to loom into view. But, by late afternoon there was still no sign of the horse thieves. Two days and nights without sleep. We were all dog-tired. We weren't going to be able to keep up this pace. And the horses were about plumb tuckered out. Pretty soon we were going to have to rest.

The sun was beginning to sink, its great red ball bleeding away on the dark razor-sharp mountain-tops when we saw them as we topped a rise. Dark silhouettes of horses and riders cantering away into the crimson haze.

'We've got 'em, boys.' I drew in my mount and leaned down to draw out my Spencer carbine. I fed my first .52 slug out of the butt stock into the breech with my trigger-guard lever and thumbed back the firing hammer. I glanced at the others. Moses and Jesus had revolvers at the ready, Tom and

Tex carbines. 'Ready? Let's go.'

We didn't give any warning, just spurred our tired broncs into one last gallop, raking blood from their sides to make them charge. At least, the others did. Paddy was all heart. He only needed a touch. He would go until he dropped. And he was fast. He was leading the field, his mane flying in my face as I hung low over his neck, my Spencer tucked into my right shoulder.

Abel Hagerty was riding out on the right wing, his slouch hat pulled low against the fierce sun's rays, his frock coat flapping as he jogged along. His *compadres* were over to his left, giving shrill yips as they urged the herd of sixty mustangs along. Hagerty turned, either heard us or saw us, and shouted a warning, swirling his mount and drawing the long-barrelled Remington. Tex fired from the saddle and his slug ripped through Hagerty's frock coat. It was a lucky shot at that distance. It was no easy feat to fire accurately from a racing mustang. But not lucky enough.

A look of alarm crossed Hagerty's crooked face and he set off for some high rocks. His sidekicks had backed away to the far side of the herd and were lost in their cloud of dust. I beckoned to Jesus, Moses and Tom to go after them, and swerved away to follow Hagerty. Tex raced alongside me. We had to stop him reaching those rocks. But he was a hundred yards off.

I hauled in, Paddy responding to me like the trained cow horse he was. I needed to take a careful shot. I aimed at Hagerty's back. Tensing in the stirrups I squeezed out the slug. Simultaneous, it seemed, with the explosion, his left arm jerked upwards. I had winged him. But, it did the trick. He spun to face us. I nudged Paddy to go on and he spurted away.

Meantime, Tex had gone charging on, true to his Texan instincts that a man must be a man. His carbine was blazing, but he was going so recklessly his bullets were going wild, chipping rocks behind Hagerty, and whining away.

The former Quantrill Raider let him come; coolly raising his Remington outstretched, he fired when he was fifty paces away, taking him out with one shot, somersaulting him off the back of his saddle.

I wasn't far behind. I gripped Paddy with my knees, steadied my carbine barrel with my left hand, and squinted along the sights as I levered in another slug. *Pa-dang*! The explosion coughed out and Hagerty ducked as the bullet whistled past his head. Like I say it wasn't easy on a plunging horse. I shouted to Paddy to 'Whoadown', and he went at a high-stepping trot, snorting with fear or anger as Hagerty traded me shot for shot. Pow-whee!

We were separated by about sixty paces now and I wanted to keep my advantage over this gunman. I had no intention of ending up like Tex. I could see Hagerty's one eye gleam with rage as he gripped his long-barrelled revolver with both hands and tried to get a bead on me. *Pow! Pang! Cha-dang!* His lead whistled past me. Close, but not close enough. Nor could I get a good aim at him as his bronc danced and circled about.

But, however good a marksman he was — and maybe in a saloon fight against him I wouldn't have stood a chance — a revolver could never be accurate at that range. And a carbine could. So I kept my distance. And I had been counting his shots. He had one left in the cylinder. We both fired together and his lead tore through my shirt sleeve.

Next, his crafty, weasel-like face registered alarm when he squeezed the trigger of his famous Remington and there was no response. And I had my seventh shot left. Maybe I should have taken him in. Called on him to surrender. If I was a Ranger I would have. But I wasn't a Ranger any more. And he was nothing but a lousy murderer and horsethief. I rode forward and deliberately fired my last bullet. His one eye bulged with fear, almost disbelief, as he jerked in his saddle and clutched at his abdomen. He looked down, saw blood pouring through his fingers and slowly slid from the saddle into the dust.

'That was for Jim Drum,' I gritted out. 'And, I guess, for Tex. And all them other soldier boys you double-executed, even if they was Yankees.'

There was a shout from behind me as Jesus came galloping up. 'Ai-yee! *Gracias por Dios, señor.* You have keeled him.'

'How about them other two varmints?'

'*Si*, they are dead, too. They ran for their lives, but we caught them. Moses, he put knife into back of Jesse Wayne, and me, I lasso and shoot Slim. No trouble.'

'Everybody OK?'

'*Si*. Everybody fine.'

'Tex caught it. He was kinda

careless.' I jumped down to take a look at him. 'He died bravely.'

'We will bury him with a cross for all to see.'

'Yeah. But the coyotes can have them other three.'

'Well, Meester Charlie, it saves us hanging them.'

'Sure does.' As Trinity Tom and Moses came cantering up dragging the other two bodies by their lariats I called, 'Good work, boys. We'll camp here tonight and head back in the morning.'

9

Our gunshots might well have attracted the attention of any wandering Apaches in the vicinity. Or even *comancheros*, come to that. This borderland was the ancient route of the heartless Mexican *bandido* gangs who came north to trade guns, liquor, or useless knick-knacks with the Comanches for stolen horses, cattle, or even abducted women and children, whom they would sell to the silver mines or brothels as slaves down in Chihuahua. So we surely ought to have set guards overnight. But we were so dog-tired after the trials of the Horsehead Trail, the stampede, the pursuit of these horsethieves and all the lack of sleep, that we neglected to. We rounded up the stolen remuda, gave our own broncs a dishful of water and a handful of split corn, chawed on cold jerky, and rolled into our blankets.

What I did do was haul up the three corpses by ropes around their necks into a manzanita tree to hang there swinging in the breeze as a warning to all horsethieves. Any nosy Apaches or Comanches would be too scared of ghosts to attack at night. And I figured to be up before dawn, which was their favourite killing time. But, to tell the truth, I was so bushed I didn't give a damn. I lay my head back on my saddle and went out like a light. The next thing I knew Jesus was shaking me by the shirt and calling, 'Hey, *señor*, wakey wakey. The birdies have been singing for two hours now.'

'Jeez!' I exploded, sitting up. 'We was lucky not to all git our throats cut. Why didn't you wake me?'

'I only just wake myself. And you sleep happy as a baby, Charlie. Here. You want coffee?'

'Is the remuda OK?'

'*Si*, everything fine. Relax.'

'Good.' I sipped at the scalding brew and caught sight, with a start,

125

of the grisly scene of the three hanging desperadoes. Their heads hanging to one side, they looked kinda peaceful. At last. 'You know, I figure there must be some bounty on them three. The last of the Quantrill Raiders.'

'Not the last,' Trinity Tom piped up. 'Jesse and Cole and them others are still alive.'

'They sho' would stink by the time we got 'em to Fort Sumner,' Moses grinned.

'Well, I ain't one to make money on former Confederates, even if they were murderous scumbags,' I said. 'So we'll leave 'em hanging.'

'I took a look in Hagerty's pockets,' Tom said. 'All he had was useless Confederate notes.'

'I guess he was looking to improve his finances,' I remarked. 'I'm purloining that natty Remington shooter of his. Anybody any objections?'

'No, *señor*.' Jesus flashed a smile. 'Iss fortunes of war.'

★ ★ ★

So, we crossed the Texas line, and drove our horses and cattle north into New Mexico following the river valley. The Pecos Plains sure was fine cattle country, carpeted with grama grass as far as the eye could see, knee high on every hill and mesa. And the wonder was that it was so sparsely populated, only perhaps, the occasional sod-buster. Indeed, the whole territory was as big as Missouri but probably contained only a few hundred Anglos at that time, and a similar number of Latinos, *peons* in their scattered adobe villages, who, twenty years before, had been colonists of Mexico, but were now very second-class US citizens. The rest were Indians, Mescaleros, hiding up in the dark mountain wall away to the west, the San Andres and Organ ranges. They were probably watching us as we passed, wondering what these men with cattle were doing coming into their ancient land.

We ambled along slowly, in no hurry, letting the cattle nip at the buds of the fine grass as they passed, so that they would look sleek and, if not fat, for a longhorn rarely looked that, at least healthy by the time we reached market. Eventually we reached about the halfway mark to Fort Sumner, the joining of the Rio Hondo, rushing down from the western mountains, with the Pecos. The water was deep and crystal clear and swarming with all manner of fish. Some former Mexicans had had the good sense to build a village here, which they called Del Rio, and they had sent the water coursing through a network of *acequias* to nourish cornfields, fruit orchards and shady cottonwood trees. It was a veritable oasis.

The *peons* were friendly in the extreme, especially when we presented them with a side of beef in exchange for baskets of peaches and melons, nuts and tortillas, eggs and lemons. Soon we were having a spontaneous *fiesta* as we sat around their village square and sampled homebrewed *aquadiente*.

'Men, you just take it easy with this firewater,' Oliver Loving warned. 'You can dance with these li'l Mex firecrackers but that's as far as it's to go. We don't want no trouble. The Spanish temperament is a jealous one and we don't want no machetes flashing. Remember these are decent people.'

'Aw, look at her showing her legs,' Trinity Tom drooled, as one of the *señoritas* swirled her dress and Jesus strutted around her, cracking his fingers, and kicking his heels, as guitars strummed and a battered cornet sounded a kind of bull-fight *pasa doble*. 'That gal's asking for it.'

It was difficult not to agree with that sentiment as the village women gathered around, smiling and flirting, even the fat mamas. And, as the night wore on, I noticed more than one 'puncher sneak off into the orchards with a dark-eyed ladyfriend. It was a fine evening of merriment and, fortunately, trouble free. They were hospitable people who simply enjoyed meeting us strangers. But those were the good days before outlaws, ne'er-do-wells and rustlers became rife in the vicinity.

In the morning, we woke to consider the fact that we were on the wrong side of the Pecos if we wished to get to Fort Sumner and we had to get the cattle across. But there we had a problem. In spite of all our halooing and whip-cracking they were in no mood to plunge down the steep banks into the rapid stream.

'What we gonna do?' Loving asked, somewhat exasperated.

'Maybe, if we took the calves across the cows would follow,' I suggested, for we had had some more recent births.

'Give it a try, Charlie.'

So I did. I went and collared Jesus, who was taking a loving farewell of a little *chiquita* — and she had such flashing eyes, if I hadn't been in love with Mary Ann I might have been tempted into sin myself.

'Come on,' I said. 'We've work to do. Round up all the calves you can find and we'll take 'em on our saddles over to the other side.'

We did so, swimming our horses against the strong surge, and scrambled them down on the far bank. The calves stood there on their spindly legs, wide-eyed and forlorn, and set up a chorus of wailing which went straight to their mothers' hearts. Those cows took to the water and swam across as fast as crocodiles, struggling up the other bank for a tender reunion. Then these mother cows became puzzled and afraid because they were separated from the main herd and set to bellowing. Hearing this, some of the younger bulls slithered down into the water, and, horns and noses raised, went paddling furiously across to join them. Maybe they thought here was their chance to start up a breakaway herd.

The older bulls watched them

indignantly, and began snorting and pawing, and it didn't need much whip cracking to send them diving into the torrent like champion swimmers determined not to let the young studs get away with this impertinence. The water cooled their ardour, however, and they forgot about fighting once they were on the other side.

The rest of the cows didn't intend hanging around on the west bank without the bulls, for their nature was to follow them, and soon the river was full of wetback cattle doing their utmost to get to the other side. Some of the more lily-livered began to panic, milling about, trying to turn back, but we swam our horses in and encouraged them with plenty of whip-cracking and shouts. Only one got swept away, and he drifted off downstream, whirling around in the current, looking back at us, plaintively. We let him go, and never did find out what happened to him.

The rest of the herd plunged and fought frantically to find a spot to climb up the opposite bank, and soon they were all back on dry land and none the worst for their dip, probably better for it, washed clean of a few more bugs.

'It worked, Charlie,' Oliver beamed. 'What would I do without you?'

'Next time we'll have to look out for a better spot to ford,' I said. 'If there is a next time.'

'Oh, there will be,' he grinned. 'This trail's gonna go down in the history books.'

'Maybe, but how we gonna get the chuck wagon across?'

Loving pushed his hat forward and scratched his grey curls. 'You got me there.'

'The oxen will swim but the wagon will sink and drown 'em. Unless — '

'Unless what? You got another bright idea?'

'If we saw down a couple of them cotton wood boughs and kinda fix them on the back. We could harness two horses behind the wagon to sorta

133

push and hold it up.'

'You mean like stretcher bearers, kinda thing?'

'That's it.'

So, we did. And, believe it or not, it worked, and, with the help of a lot of hauling on ropes, we had the wagon on the other side by noon. We'd removed most of the perishables, the flour, salt, and so forth, plus the ammunition, and wrapped them in tarpaulin to portage them across. We were home and dry. Mind you, old Sonuvabitch Stevens sure looked uncomfortable as he sat holding the reins, up to his waist in turbulent water going 'Giddy-yap!' We all had a good laugh at his expense.

'There's another invention you oughta patent, Charlie,' Oliver told me. 'A horse-powered water wagon for Sunday jaunts.'

For a moment I thought he might be serious. 'Come on,' I scowled. 'Get those wet bedrolls out. You can drape them over the back of your broncs to dry them out as we move along. Let's get this show on the road.'

★ ★ ★

We were nearly there. Only another sixty or so miles to go to the fort where we hoped to sell at least part of the herd. I had pencilled a letter to Mary Ann while the boys were whooping it up back at our little *fiesta*. *'The trail's gone well,'* I wrote. *'We had some trouble with three Johnny Rebs who got fresh and had to shoot the sonsuvbitches. This is fine country. I'm staying faithful to you, Mary Ann, and think about you every day, when I got time, that is. I hope you ain't letting that Gideon Claypole sit on your porch and hold your hand. Soon as we sell these cows I'm coming back to marry you, honey. Your ever-loving Charlie.'*
It was a cheerful surprise to see a platoon of cavalry come jogging along the riverbank towards us, the sun glinting on their rattling sabres,

the Stars and Bars rippling in the breeze. They drew up alongside us and their lieutenant asked us where we were from. 'Fort Belknap, Texas,' I told him.

'Had any trouble?'

'Nope, apart from Comanch', drought, hossthieves and stampede. Just the usual.'

'We're heading for Fort Belknap ourselves, carrying dispatches.'

'Hey,' I called, pulling my letter out of my wallet. 'Could you see that this gets sent onto Freedom for me? I'll give you the quarter postage.'

'That's OK,' he winked. 'I'll send it official mail.'

'Don't forget,' I shouted, as they started away. 'It's for my fy-an-cee.'

* * *

No trouble? An hour after the troopers had passed I looked across the river and thought I saw movement, a horse-rider loping along through the tall grass.

And he wasn't wearing no shirt, nor pants. And he had feathers twisted in his long hair. One horse-rider? No, several. They were bounding along the crest of the bank, coming out of the trees behind him, and staring across at us, brandishing spears and longarms in their hands. Correct that: not several, about thirty of the varmints.

'Injins,' I yelled, riding up to the point to join Loving, and pulling my carbine from the cinch. I raised it to my shoulder thinking a few shots might scare them off.

'What you doing?' Oliver yelled. 'You want another stampede on our hands?'

I lowered the Spencer and thought about that. The Indians had ridden well up ahead of us and with blood-curdling screams were already leaping their ponies into the river and swimming them across. 'What you gonna do? We better hit 'em while we got a chance.'

'No, Charlie. That ain't always the

best way. We can parley. See what they want.'

'See what they want? What they want is our scalps and our cows.'

'They ain't wearing paint. The Mescaleros 're supposed to be at peace.'

'This lot,' I yelped, as the half-naked savages came charging down the bank towards us, 'don't look partic'ly peaceful.'

'Let's go meet 'em,' Oliver said, and spurred his stallion forward, while I, somewhat reluctantly, followed.

It took the wind out of the Messies' sails for they pulled in their broncs in a scuffle of dust twenty paces from us, and started shouting and grimacing, frenziedly thrusting their weapons at the sky. One, who seemed to be their leader, wearing a kind of waistcoat of feathers and little else, with a strong, hooked nose and fierce eyes, beckoned to them to quieten down, thrust his head forward and spat out some guttural words.

'What's he going on about?' Oliver asked.

'From what little Apache I know it seems he's telling us we can't pass, that this is his land.'

The chief was, indeed, waving his palm back and forth to accentuate this. And then he began pointing with a finger at the cows as they began to trundle past, one, two, three . . . up to ten. And tapping his dark chest.

'The durn cheek of it. He wants us to give him ten as a kind of toll.' I leaned forward in my saddle and scowled back at him. 'You thievin' redskins can git outa our way. Or else. You see this' — I cocked the Spencer and raised it, pointing it at one, two, three, four of his men, going 'Bang! Bang! Bang! Bang! I can shoot seven of you down in the time it takes you to reload one of them dang single shots.' I tried to roughly translate this to him in 'Pache, as his braves angrily skittered their ponies away, and turned back, raising their lances and ancient rifles in readiness.

'That's enough, Charlie,' Oliver shouted, and raised his own hands, trying to calm them down as our boys rode up to gather around us. 'What you trying to do, start a massacre?'

'You ain't gonna let them rob us of our cows?'

The chief was pointing to his mouth and to his belly, saying something about his people being hungry.

It occurred to me that the boys were only wearing sidearms, their carbines being stashed away in the wagon, and that had gone on up ahead. If it came to a fight we weren't going to do so well. We were likely to lose most of our men and have the herd stampeded into the bargain. Maybe Loving was talking sense.

'OK,' I said, 'let's talk about this.' I pulled a pouch of baccy from my shirt and tossed it to the chief. He was a handsome man for an aboriginal, his body lithe and muscled, with that strange coppery burnish they have.

His ornaments around his neck, arms, ankles, and dangling from his ears, were well made. A cut-up on the Comanche, you might say, but they're the ugliest-looking bunch in the world. 'A pity we didn't bring a few gew-gaws to fob them off with.'

The chief took the baccy and smelt it. Then raised his arm to his mouth like drinking from a bottle. 'Tah-kee-lah,' he said.

'Nope. We ain't got none of that. It ain't good for ya. We give you five cows' — I indicated with my hand — 'take them and go.'

At this, the Indians started screaming and scowling and waving their weapons again, broiling for a fight. They knew they'd got us scared and at a disadvantage.

The chief drew himself up and raised both hands, fingers outstretched. And made a chopping sign with his palm. End of argument.

'Give him ten, Charlie,' Oliver said. It's always hard for a Texan to back down. It's the way we've been raised. We don't back down to no man, especially not an Indian. I pointed my carbine at the chief and muttered, 'He gets it first. He won't fight. He don't want to risk the wrath of the military.'

The chief glowered at me, and Oliver muttered, 'I wouldn't be so sure. Is it worth that gamble?'

'I dunno. Maybe, as they say, discretion is better than valour.' I slowly lowered the carbine, turned my paint, and beckoned to him, riding over to the herd and cutting out first one, then another decent-sized beef, and running it out to them, until they'd got a group of ten. 'There,' I said. 'Take 'em and go.'

They gave whoops and three of them leapt down, drawing their long knives, which flashed in the sun, and a beast collapsed. They butchered it there and then, cutting steaks, which they tossed to their mates, who sat there hungrily chewing, like wolves, blood streaming down their necks. They hung the rest over their ponies' backs. The chief raised an arm to us, shouted something, and led them away, herding the other nine cattle with them.

'I guess,' I said, as I watched them go, 'they did once kinda own this land.'

10

The adobe walls of Fort Summer were flushed pink and purple by the westering sun as we approached. To us it looked like the holy city of Jerusalem after our long trail. As we chivvied our long line of cattle along we began to see signs of Navajos. There were 8,000 of them settled in the territory, centred around their reservation at the Bosque Redondo. They had put up a vicious fight against American incursion until, in the Civil War, Colonel Kit Carson's cannons and burnt-earth policy had starved and beaten them into submission. Now here they were, their one bitter complaint that they had been forcibly removed from their sacred land.

We brought the cattle to a halt and left them under guard as Loving and I rode into the fort to negotiate a deal.

Around the gates outside were a few ragged Navajo women with baskets of trinkets to sell. They were very clever with their hands and made handsome silver and bluestone jewellery. One had fashioned a lantern-holder from a discarded can of oysters. Another, with a baby at her breast, ran forward, her hand outstretched. She indicated by fingers to her mouth that they were hungry, so I took a look at the arm bangle she was offering me.

'She seems to be saying it'll bring you good fortune,' Oliver laughed. 'Though it don't seem to have done a lot for her.'

'I would buy it for Mary Ann,' I said, 'but all I got is Confederate dollars and they ain't much good to her or anybody.'

'Here.' Oliver flipped her a dollar. 'I'll buy it for you as a wedding present.'

'Gee, thanks,' I said, and clipped it on my wrist for the time being. It was a perfect fit. Maybe that should have told me something.

Inside the dusty fort, there was a wide parade ground with spacious officers' houses, and the men's quarters cramped in among the stables on the other side. When in a few years' time the Navajos would be returned to their own lands, the fort would be closed down and sold to the Maxwell family. It subsequently became the hang-out for riffraff and bandits like Billy the Kid, who, after a brief but colourful career in which he gunned down twenty-two men, was killed here by lawman Pat Garrett. But that's another story. At this moment I'm talking about, Billy would have been a six-year-old kid running around the streets of the Kansan cowtown of Washita with his Irish-Brooklyn mama, who probably thought what a sweet li'l feller he was!

However, I digress. Mr Loving was hot to see the commanding officer, a Colonel Pierce, who presented himself, big and bustling with bushy mutton-chop whiskers. Yes, he would be more than keen on behalf of the government to purchase our stock, but only the steers and bulls. They would be slaughtered and supplied to the reservation.

Oliver Loving was none too pleased at that. He had hoped to sell the complete herd. So he held out for a good price. The colonel blustered, but agreed. It was, after all, not his money: the taxpayers footed the bill. We sealed the deal over a sup of whiskey and it never tasted so good.

'Gentlemen, would you like to dine with us in the officers' mess tonight? If so, you might care to use the facilities of our bath house.' His nose twitched as he looked us over. 'And the sutler's store where you can purchase clean clothing.'

What a blessing it was to soak in a barrel of hot soapy suds and wash away the trail dust while a Mexican woman scrubbed my jeans and blue canvas shirt and hung them out to dry. With two fingers to her nose she pitched my long johns and socks into the rubbish box, so Oliver treated me to a new set. And I had my thatch cut and my beard trimmed by a Mex barber as I splashed and sang about my 'Sweet Texas Rose'.

We might have still looked like sage rats, but we certainly smelled sweeter when we presented ourselves at the colonel's place for dinner. His wife received us graciously, a fragile little body, who looked like she'd be more at home among the tinkly teacups of Boston society. Instead, she was keeping the flag flying in this far-flung outpost.

It was mighty strange to be back in polite company, eating fine vittles with our legs under a table, using silver tableware, instead of squatting round a smoky campfire amid rowdy cowboys.

'My husband is awfully pleased to see you,' Mrs Pearce said, in her fluttery voice. 'The Indians are so distressed and starving. We haven't been able to meet our commitment

148

to supply them with beef.'

'My wife was worried we might have a rebellion on our hands like up in Minnesota,' Pearce grunted, his mouth full of potatoes. 'I've told her that ain't likely to happen again.'

'It was only four years ago,' she said, with a shudder. 'So horrible.'

She was referring, of course, to the uprising by the Santee Sioux when their promised rations were not forthcoming. Women had been gang-raped, children slaughtered, men tortured, 600 settlers killed in one day of bloodlust. The biggest massacre of civilians in the history of the nation. For a week the fort had been under attack, the town of New Ulm besieged. When armed relief arrived the uprising fizzled out as quickly as it began. And in the biggest mass hanging ever seen thirty-one Indians paid with their lives. Most folk spoke about it in hushed voices, as if it was something they preferred to forget.

'No need to worry about the Indians

around here, ma'am,' Oliver Loving said. 'Now we've blazed this trail there'll be more herds of beef coming into New Mexico than have ever before been seen.'

'You Texans must have suffered badly from Comanche attacks' — Mrs Pearce seemed to have Indian cruelties on her mind. 'Weren't you attacked on your way here? Aren't they the most savage of the tribes? You lost a friend, didn't you, Mr Goodnight? How you must hate them.'

'No, I don't hate them, ma'am. From an early age they are trained for war. That's their way of life. They've been fighting the Spanish for four hundred years and now they're fighting us. We're sworn enemies, that's all. I've seen farms burned, families massacred, but I don't hate them. I respect their cunning, their courage, their horsemanship. I kill them, because it's either that or be killed. They give no quarter. I certainly wouldn't want to fall into their hands alive. They have some nasty methods with prisoners. But I still don't hate them. I guess if I was in their shoes I'd do the same thing: fight for my land. But, I ain't. I'm on t'other side.'

'Are you really trying to tell us,' one of the officers piped up, 'that these Comanche aren't really bad sorts, that they have some tender qualities?'

'Well, even a wolf is tender with his young,' I said, wishing I hadn't got into this, as I wasn't doing my share of eating, and an orderly had whipped away my unfinished meal. 'I don't know whether you've heard of that girl, Cynthia Ann Parker? A little blonde girl with blue eyes, aged nine, when the Comanche raided Parker's Fort on Novasota Creek in '36. They made quick butchery of most everyone inside, but stole her away.'

'Yes, I heard about that,' Mrs Pearce said. 'Poor little thing. Her family searched for her for years afterwards, didn't they?'

'That's right, ma'am. She was seen once four years later, when she was thirteen, in a Comanche camp on the Canadian River by Colonel Len Williams. He offered to ransom her, but the offer was rejected. He only had a trader and a guide with him so he couldn't take her by force. The girl was allowed to sit, Indian fashion, before him, but she refused to answer his questions.'

'So, what happened to her?' the colonel asked.

'She wasn't seen again by a white man for fifteen years, and by that time she had married a Qwahadi Comanche chief, and had two halfbreed children. A party of white hunters visited her camp and spoke to her. Cynthia Ann told them she did not want to return with them. She was happy as she was. She was a Comanche.'

'Just a minute,' the lieutenant put in. 'I've no wish to ruin a good story, but aren't you the Texas Ranger — Goodnight — the man who rescued her? I read something about it in the journals.'

'I helped. Five years ago I was riding with Cap'n Sul Ross and Cap'n Jack Cureton and a troop of the Rangers when we surprised her village. There was a melée, and Captain Ross was aiming at a fleeing Indian woman. The wind blew aside her blanket and I saw that she was white. I shouted to Ross to hold his fire. It was Cynthia Ann, all right. Her husband, the chief, and his two sons, were away hunting, but she had another child in her arms. She begged and pleaded with us to be allowed to stay where she was, but it was decided I should take her back. That's how come I got credited with rescuing her.'

'And was she all right?' Mrs Pearce asked. 'Did she settle down?'

'No, she didn't. I took her back to the Texas settlements and she was identified by her uncle, Colonel Isaac Parker. But she could hardly speak any English, and was sullen, like she was a captive. Two or three times she escaped and tried to reach the Comanches, but each time she was captured and brought back.'

'So what happened to her?'

'I wrote to her aunt about her, and she replied that Cynthia Ann's baby, Topsannah, had died in 1864, and after that, she refused to eat and starved herself to death. I reckon she just died of a broken heart.'

Mrs Pearce wiped a tear from her eye corner and murmured, 'That's very sad.'

'Yes, but the reason I told you that is by way of pointing out that if a white girl, with her upbringing, should become so damn fond of them, Comanches can't be all bad, can they?'

Colonel Pearce tried to change the subject to one more cheerful, such as the progress being made now on the cross-continental railroad. Currently, 30,000 Chinese coolies were labouring to cross the most precipitous part of The Rockies.

'On the one hand you've got aboriginals still living in the Stone Age, and on the other a modern thrusting civilization, gunboats on the Mississippi, men conquering the sky in hot air balloons, and someone has just invented a dynamo to create instant electrical current. There is bound to be conflict, and I'm afraid the day of the Indian is fast disappearing.'

Me, I'd never seen a railroad engine, a balloon or gunboat, and, apart from drawings in the journals, I had as little idea about them as the Comanche. That the sun never set on the British Empire, and that sailing ships were daily transporting thousands of immigrants to our country to escape the Irish famine and the ghettos of Europe, I was aware. But, as far as civilization was concerned I had an uneasy feeling I preferred to live as far from it as possible. The only place I was happy was on a horse under the wide-open Western skies.

With her predeliction for the gloomy,

Mrs Pearce punctured her husband's rhetoric by pointing out that immigrants brought disease, that Asiatic cholera had killed 200 in London, was now sweeping across America and had reached Kansas.

'In that case,' I said to Loving, 'it's a good job we decided to come this way.'

'Why don't you go and read your new book *War and Peace*, dear,' Pearce said. 'While I pass the whiskey round among the men?'

When she had gone, he raised his eyes to the ceiling, as much as to say, 'Ain't I hampered?' It struck me that marriage ain't always what it's cracked up to be, especially if a man gets hitched to a pain in the rear like Mrs Pearce. Thank goodness I had a sparky soul like Mary Ann waiting for me.

Over the whiskey, Pearce asked, 'How do you boys want your payment? By cheque, dollar notes or gold?'

'Gold,' Oliver quickly replied. 'Them

flimsy bits of paper are prone to get blown away on the wind.'

'In that case' — the colonel scribbled a note — 'you can take this over to the bursar's office as soon as you've finished your drink. Here's the best of luck to you boys.'

'And you, sir,' Oliver said. 'I guess I'll drive the cows and calves on up to Denver. There's hungry miners up there and ranchers wanting to stock their land. Are you coming with me, Charlie?'

'Waal, I would,' I hesitated, 'but I'm in a terrible hurry to get back to Texas.'

'I kinda guessed you were,' he laughed, and winked at the others. 'The boy's in lurve! So we'd better not waste time, gents.'

When we had left them, he said to me, 'You know, once this news gets out there's gonna be an influx of drovers up here, and prices are bound to fall. I suggest while I'm away you go back and quickly get another herd together, and I'll rejoin you, and we'll do this again.'

'That's fine by me, if Mary Ann don't mind.' I was still feeling guilty about not going with him. 'I'd love to see Colorado, but my ears have been burning like fire. I've a feeling Mary Ann's father and that lousebag Claypole have been nagging her, telling her it's time she got wed to a nice respectable townsman, and it ain't no good her waiting for that no-good wandering cowboy Charlie Goodnight. I can feel her sticking up for me, but the other ear's getting the best of it, and I'm certain they're beating her down. So, I better be going. I might already be too late: I couldn't bear to live without that little filly.'

'On your horse, Charlie, and ride like hell. But, first, we've got to go to the bursar's office and get this cheque cashed.'

I could hardly believe my eyes when the little soldier in the office opened a big safe and started counting out gold twenty-dollar pieces. And counting . . . and counting. Oliver put his palm through it and pushed across my share.

'All that?' I stuttered.

'Eight cents a pound for all the steers. And I'll pay you for your share of the cows and calves. By my arithmetic that makes twelve thousand dollars. You arguing?'

'No . . . no . . . I ain't arguing. Kinda surprised, thassall.' I called over to the soldier clerk. 'I don't s'pose you got a gunny sack I can put this in? Or maybe two?'

Oliver laughed and slapped me on the back. 'Charlie, I think we made the right decision. We must do this again, boy.'

The men were mighty pleased with their $20 bonus on top of their wages, and quickly resorted to a little ramshackle *cantina* an enterprising Mexican had built outside the gates of the fort. I slipped Jesus an extra $20 'eagle', seeing as he was my right-hand man.

'You going on up to Denver?' I asked, as we sipped some tequila and sucked on lemon slices to keep away the scurvy.

'No, I go back to Mexico to see my mama and sister. I ride with you, Charlie.'

'Me, too,' Moses grinned, who had kinda attached himself to me like a mongrel dog.

'Well, you better be ready to ride hard' — I dashed back the tequila and got to my feet — 'because I'm leaving right now. I ain't got no time to lose.'

As we climbed on our broncs and headed back south, leading a packjack with my gold on his back, I could still hardly believe my luck. It had occurred to me to share my $12,000 with the others. But, hell, this was the difference between being the boss of the outfit and just one of the boys.

★ ★ ★

We had no trouble on the way back except that at one point I lost my gold. We had taken a short rest midday on the banks of the Pecos and it was so hot we kinda dozed off. I woke with a start, and, looking round, saw the mule was gone. Oh, no! My heart sank into my boots. Had some Injin sneaked up and stole him? Or had he dragged his ground-hitching and wandered off, took it in his head to go visit some distant relatives? I spent a frantic hour searching for him, until I heard a raucous bray and found him having an altercation with a bobcat in a ravine. $12,000 in gold was still on his back, thank my lucky stars.

That night I tossed and turned in my soogans wondering, feverishly, what Mary Ann was up to, whether she might be doing those things to Claypole she used to do to me. My own beanpole wasn't giving me any rest. 'Come on,' I shouted, as I jumped up at 3 a.m. 'Let's ride. We ain't got no time to lose.'

11

We all three were worn and weary from travelling when we rode into Freedom as I hadn't even let us stop for a bite to eat that day. Something was niggling at me to hurry. Moses and Jesus headed for the saloon and I rode on down to Pfout's Emporium. A cleaning lady was locking up and I called, 'What's it closed for?' and she said, 'Ain't you heard? They're gettin' married.'

'Who is?' My heart fell for I already knew the answer. '*She* is? Where?'

'Down at the church, of course.'

Well, you could have knocked me down with a feather. I was so stunned, I just sort of sat there for a few seconds, and then hauled poor old Paddy hard round and galloped off down the wide dust road between the false fronts, dragging my mule and $12,000 in gold along behind. The church was a big white-painted clapboard place with a tall spire looking down on the street. I always thought it had a kind of condemning air.

But that didn't deter me. I could hear the euphonium parping away at 'Here Comes the Bride', or some such song, so I raised Paddy on his back legs and had him smash in the door with his forehooves, and we clattered inside, still dragging the moke. Old biddies screamed, and men in black, with hymn books in their hands turned to stare indignantly. I guess they thought I must be drunk or crazy, or both.

Mary Ann, in a white satin dress, was standing in front of the altar alongside that dude, Claypole. And he was pushing a ring on her finger, and embracing her, kissing my gal in front of all those people.

The minister, a pinch-nosed old creep, intoned, 'I pronounce you man and wife,' just as I burst in.

'Wait a minute,' I shouted. 'You cain't do that.'

Mr Pfout stepped out into the aisle and tried to hang onto my gallumphing horse. He had gone more beetroot red than ever before and held up his Bible like I was the very Devil. 'Get out of here, Goodnight,' he shouted. 'You're too late.'

'Charlie!' Mary Ann yelled, holding her veil aside. 'What in tarnation you doin' here?'

'You promised to marry me, Mary Ann. I come as fast as I could all the way from Fort Sumner.'

'You ain't writ me. Why should I want to marry an ornery, bow-legged prairie bum who ain't got a dime? And what's that face fuzz you got?'

'Didn't you get my letter, Mary Ann?' I realized I did look a bit of a sage rat in my battered Lone Star hat, horn-tattered chaps, worn-out boots with one sole flapping, strung with iron, and straddling a dusty pinto, with an angry lop-eared eared moke alongside, but what the hell! 'Didn't the lootenant pass it onto you?'

'What lootenant? I ain't had no letter.' Mary Ann hung onto the arm of Claypole, in his natty grey suit with silver facings. 'Gideon's mayor of this boro' now.'

'Good for him,' I snarled.

At this point the mule decided to leave his calling card, a big steaming pile, and Mary Ann wailed, 'Charlie, you dunghead, why do you want to spoil my wedding?'

'So you're married?'

'Yes, I'm married.'

'Well, I'm sorry, Mary Ann,' I said. 'I shoulda got here a day sooner. I wish you all happiness, and you, Mr Claypole.'

I turned my animals, touched my hat to the congregation, and rode out of there. At the door I heard Mary Ann shriek, 'Oh, Charlie, you dumbcluck! You allus causin' trouble.'

I rode back up to the saloon. Jesus and Moses were just about to split a bottle. I took it from them and filled myself a tumblerful. I downed it in one, and filled another.

'What's wrong, *amigo*? I thought you were going to get married?'

'Too late,' I gasped, as the whiskey hit me. 'Too late by two seconds.'

I sat the rest of the night staring into my whiskey as Jesus and Moses caroused with the 'soiled doves'. Somehow, I couldn't join them. It wouldn't have been right, somehow, on Mary Ann's wedding night.

In the morning light I staggered out, my legs a tad unsteady. My mule, gold and hoss had gone. But I discovered Moses had had the sense to take them down to the livery, and he was sleeping in the hay with his head propped on the sacks of gold coin. Jesus came wandering in after me, his gunbelt hung over his shoulder.

'Boys,' I said, patting his bald head. 'I ain't the first man to have loved and lost, nor likely to be the last, but I ain't spending the rest of my life looking at the world through the bottom of a bottle. Jesus, you'll have to postpone your vacation. We got work to do. Another herd to raise. I'll just deposit most of this stuff over at the bank while you have some breakfast. Then we'll ride, OK?'

Jesus gave a shrill Spanish holler, 'Ai, yai, yai! Thass OK by me, boss.'

And Moses gave a big grin. 'Me, too,' he said.

12

By the time Oliver Loving got back from Denver we had put together another herd, paying gold this time, at rock bottom Texas prices, but ensuring that we only had superior grade mature beeves. Consequently, we lost only five on our second trip on the Horsehead Trail even though the sun burned just as fierce. And we sold at a good profit.

When 1867 opened we could see that our monopoly of the Pecos valley market was ended. Several outfits were making plans to push cattle over the waterless trail, including my old Ranger pal, Captain Jack Cureton. So Loving told me we would put another bunch together and drive them all the way to Colorado for the stocker market. I didn't argue. He was the business brain. And I had come to rely on his advice, and, to tell the truth, had come almost to regard him as a substitute father. All I wanted to do was throw myself into my work and forget Mary Ann.

One day he saw me looking mean and moody, and he said, 'You know, it ain't my piece to say anything against that filly, but, you know, I've bumped into her and she strikes me as being real flighty. She's leading that Claypole a merry dance. Maybe it was best you didn't marry her, you being away all the time on long trail drives; you'd be torturing yourself wondering what the hell she was getting up to.'

I was about to fire up, resentfully, but I marked what he said, and remembered how it was true I'd often seen Mary Ann, when we were courting, flirting with other fellas and breaking off surreptitious conversations when I appeared.

'Maybe,' I said, 'you got a point. Maybe it's true, I'm better off without her.'

'Maybe you are. Take the advice of a happily married man, Charlie. I know females are almighty scarce out on the prairie, but just you bide your time and you'll meet one. You're a man who deserves a good woman you can trust and rely on, and I wouldn't mind betting one of these days you'll find her.'

'Maybe,' I growled, and rode off. But it was a comforting thought.

* * *

Early in the year as we put together a herd, it looked like we were getting into a race with the other outfits. And there was also unmistakable sign on the trail that Indians were out. The Comanches had learned of our activities and were lurking in the Horsehead country to try to take their pickings. We divided our cattle into two bunches and had our men ride with carbines at the ready. We knew that another drover called Jim Burleson had his herd already in front of us, and Captain Cureton's was behind us as we set off for the Middle Concho. Twice we were attacked by Comanche raiding parties but we beat them off. One of our herders caught an arrow in his head and I had to get out my pliers again. I sent him back to his mother to be nursed.

The army was busy building a new fort on the Concho and on the way there we found a German who had been killed and scalped on the trail. And we heard that a group of gold miners had fought a brisk skirmish with the same band. News also came through that a war party had killed a man and wounded a woman at the new Horsehead Crossing trading post. Things weren't looking too good.

'There's nothing we can do but go on,' Loving told me. He was a strange mixture of a man, generally cool-headed and inclined to caution, but under fire this man of strong religious instincts became fiery-tempered and foolishly brave. He would charge right up to a body of Comanche and fire his repeating rifle into them, charge right through them, circle round and do the same again. He would take on the whole Comanche nation rather than lose his herd.

When we sat around the campfire at night, listening to the eerie howls out in the brush, he confided to me that he had a premonition this was going to be a real bad trip. 'I'm sorry I got you into it, Charlie,' he said. 'I've gotten too gold greedy.'

'Aw,' I said. 'We ain't gonna let a few Comanch' stop us.'

The strange thing was that this time we had no trouble with thirsty cattle. The rain bucketed down every day until we reached the Horsehead crossing. The 'long dry trail' became a march of slippery sliding mud through which we resolutely tramped, water coursing from our hat brims and streaming down our slickers. We sat around our fire at night miserable and sodden. The rain made the cattle nervous, too, and ready to run.

'Stampede!' The dreaded cry was howled out just as I was crawling out of my soogans in a grey mist of dawn on the west bank of the Pecos where I bedded down our first herd. I grabbed my carbine and leaped on the nearest mustang. I didn't need to shout any instructions. The thundering of hooves of a thousand beeves on the run told us all we needed to know. We had to get after them, try to turn them, try to slow them. It was poor visibility, hissing rain in our eyes, but as we galloped after them we heard the unmistakable screaming of Comanches and glimpsed their naked, glistening bodies dashing along at the front of the herd, urging them on. 'Don't shoot,' I hollered to the men, for I didn't want to make the beeves go any faster, if that was possible. And, anyway, it would have been like trying to shoot fish in water. We whirled our slickers and galloped along breakneck driving into the herd behind the Indians, and watched them go as we gradually, after a mile or so, brought the rest to a bawling, restless halt.

Speechless with rage, I watched the Comanches disappear into the mist. When we made a rough count it looked like they had got away with 300 head.

Bad news greeted me when I rode back to see how the second herd under Loving was faring. He, too, was fuming, his camp in disarray. The Comanches had attacked and escaped with the largest part of the herd, near on a thousand head. In his anger, he had shot at the Comanches which had only made things worse. They had had a hell of a job to save any cattle at all.

'We've got to do something about this,' he shouted at me through the din, as his cowboys rode back and forth. 'I'm going to ride to Fort Sumner to see if I can't get a platoon of troopers to come help us out.'

'That's a crazy idea, Oliver,' I yelled,

174

equally angry. 'It's dangerous country to go through. There's Indians lurking everywhere.'

'It's only two hundred miles, Charlie. I'll make it. And I'll tell you another reason why I gotta go: the beef schedules are going to be awarded in June and I gotta get there before these other damn outfits do and tell them we're on our way.'

'It's a foolish idea. Who's being reckless now? Have a cup of coffee, Oliver,' I told him. 'Simmer down. Think this over.'

'I don't want a cup of cawfee,' he bellowed. 'Don't you understand, we're short of time? You follow along with the herds, and make it fast. I'll take One-armed Bill Wilson and we'll be back afore you've missed us. Where's a fresh bronc? Where's Wilson?'

'You aren't travelling by daylight, surely? Have you lost your senses, Oliver? Travel by night, hide out by day, thass the way to do it.'

'Aw, you're as jittery as an old maid,'

he said, and bustled about getting his horse saddled and some hard rations, stuffing a box of bullets in his suit pocket. He swung aboard, and saluted me, giving a reckless grin. 'We ain't got time to wait for darkness.'

He lashed his mount and went speeding away, followed by Wilson in his Stetson and flapping duster. I watched them go, but I didn't like it. It was the first time I'd fallen out with my partner.

* * *

On the third afternoon out, I later discovered, my warnings were justified. A large raiding party of Comanche appeared and chased the two men hard towards the Pecos. As they reached the steep cliffsides of the river, their mounts were shot from under them. These Comanche were equipped with the latest carbines. Loving and One-armed Bill took cover in the cane-brakes and drove the Indians back with their lead. But one, cleverer than the rest, slipped through a growth of polecat bush. The Comanche's bullet broke Loving's wrist and bored into his side. Wilson's shot killed the Indian, and darkness descended to save the besieged men.

My friend, the cattleman, was bleeding badly and begged One-armed Bill to save himself. Wilson agreed to try in the hope he could find help and return. He climbed down to the Pecos at moonrise, discarded his boots and clothing, except for his vest and long johns, and tried to swim the river, holding his rifle in his one hand. It was impossible. He nearly drowned. So he abandoned it and floated along the bankside on the current. At one point he saw a Comanche searching the riverbank, but he hid under some smartweeds and escaped. At dawn he waded ashore, and, barefoot, headed back towards our trail herd. He walked for three days across the prairie flats until he saw our dust.

That was when we saw him, nearly naked, exhausted, tottering towards us on his bleeding feet. He collapsed when we reached him, but gradually croaked out his story. Immediately, we jumped on our broncs and went hell for leather to search for Loving. But my partner had disappeared.

When we reached Fort Sumner, to our joy we found the cattleman hobbling around. His sunburned face was wreathed in happy wrinkles as he told us how he had dragged himself for five miles after One-arm Bill departed. For five days he had hidden in a narrow gap in the cliff without food. When he saw some Mexicans passing he hailed them, and, for $150, they agreed to take him to Fort Sumner. 'They wanted two hundred, but I beat them down,' he grinned.

The next day I went to visit him at the fort and found that he had had a relapse. A surgeon, who had never carried out such an operation, had removed his wounded arm. It had become infected and he was in a bad way. I could see from his eyes that he knew he was dying.

'I'm worried about my wife and family, Charlie. Would you continue our partnership until there's enough to care for them?'

It was a strange request but I readily promised to do so. 'Go to Colorado, Charlie,' Oliver Loving coughed out just before he died. 'It's God's own country. An' you'll make your fortune.'

We buried him in the fort alongside a row of graves of other officers killed by Indians. I'm not a man who often weeps, but that day by his graveside bitter tears flowed.

13

I took Loving's advice and herded the cattle he and I had brought through at such cost on up to Denver. I remembered him telling me about a tough old guy called Uncle Dick Wootton who stood guard with a shotgun at Raton Pass claiming that the road he had built was a toll road. The ornery old buzzard had the nerve to ask ten cents a head for cattle passing over the mountain pass.

'Go to hell,' I told him.

We left him dancing with rage as we turned our cattle and sought a new route. We found a promising way through Trincheras Pass and blazed a new trail, forcing the cattle through that virgin land. We actually cut 100 miles off the distance to Pueblo. It was the trail that all the herds followed afterwards and put poor old Dick out of business!

Colorado certainly was beautiful country, with its rolling parkland on the slopes of the mountains, and the snow-clad peaks of The Rockies climbing away into the distance. But I remembered my promise and returned to Texas. By the following year I had $80,000 in the bank. Of this I turned $40,000 over to Mrs Loving, and bought out my stepbrother, J W Steeck for $20,000.

'You know, Charlie,' he said, with a rueful grin. 'I reckon I was wrong when I said that Horsehead Trail would never pay.'

With the remaining $20,000 and the cattle of the CV brand I went back into business for myself.

It was about this time that a Texas rancher called John Chisum came looking for me. He was very interested in what I had to tell him about the new trail through Horsehead Crossing and the fine grassland in the Pecos

Valley. He was a big man with a face like hewn mahogany, stone-steady eyes watching me from beneath the brim of his tall Stetson. He didn't say much, or give away what he was thinking, but plied us with drink and got us talking. I had an uneasy feeling I couldn't trust him, but not in a bad way. Just that he was a very astute man and would cut anybody's throat in business if he had the chance.

'Look here,' he said. 'I'd be willing to pay you well if you gathered a herd together and took them up through there for me. I'll provide the drovers to go with you and pay their wages. And I'll pay you over the top what you would get if you sold the herd for slaughter.'

'What do we do with the cows, then?' I asked.

'You just leave them to fatten up on that grass you describe where the Rio Hondo meets the Pecos. My men will stay and guard them.'

'What you gonna do with them?'

'I dunno,' he shrugged. 'I ain't sure yet. Can you do this for me?'

It wasn't what I wanted, but he was offering a very good deal. So, over the next two years I herded him up about 4,000 head of longhorns and left them to run in that valley tended by his men. They had built themselves a log cabin bunkhouse, stables and corrals, but it looked like just a temporary set-up. On the last trip Chisum, himself, rode with us.

'So, what now?' I asked, after he had paid me off.

'You go back to Texas and just keep the cattle coming, Charlie,' he said. 'I'll be waiting for you.'

It seemed a reasonable arrangement. Having lost the gal I loved I was in no hurry to settle down, and I was footloose and fancy free. But I kicked myself afterwards that I had not had some sort of partnership agreement drawn up with Chisum. At the back of my mind I was planning to stash enough cash in the bank so I could afford a good piece of land when the time came.

Before going back to Texas I rode a ride up the Hondo tributary to see what the country was like and came across a herd of cows being run by an Irishman near the township of Lincoln. And clearly visible on their hides was my CV brand. These 700 cows must have been the ones the Comanche had run off from us!

'Whadda ya know!' I said. The Irishman blustered and claimed to have paid a Texan cattle dealer for them. He flatly refused to make any recompense. So I wasted a lot of time taking out a private summons against him. It was a matter, I thought, of principle. Jeez! I must have been naïve.

The case was heard in court at the town of Las Vegas which is at the north end of the Pecos Valley with the great plains rolling off to the east and the Sangre de Cristo mountains rising in rugged splendour behind it to the west. Las Vegas, however, was a cess pool of corruption. The so-called judge threw my case out, claiming there was insufficient proof, and had the nerve to fine me $75 costs. The Irishman obviously had friends in high places.

I can assure you after that experience I rarely bothered consulting lawyers or lawmen. I made my own law and was ready to enforce it at the point of a gun. If somebody stole my cows I went after them and took them back. And if anybody argued, they didn't stay alive long enough to make out any complaints. That was the way it had to be. I was getting older and getting harder and tougher every day. I liked to deal fairly with people, and if they were straight with me everything was fine. If they weren't, well, we had a falling out.

I still hadn't got myself a spread and for the next few years I continued working as a kind of freelance cattle drover for John Chisum. I must have been blind not to see what he was doing: taking over the whole of the

Pecos Valley was his grand plan. Pretty soon I had herded up 10,000 longhorns from Texas for him.

At the end of my last trip through, I asked him what exactly he was going to do. 'I'm going to move this herd up to the Bosque Redondo now the Navajo have gone,' he drawled, 'and you're going to help me.'

I did what he asked, helped move that immense body of cattle. People still talk about that great migration. It was strung out for miles on the trail, and when it was bedded down at night it required the night riders three hours to walk their horses around it.

This was the beginning of the famous Jingle Bob and Long Rail brands, the nucleus of an empire that by 1876 would have multiplied to 80,000 head of longhorns ranging on rich grasslands from old Fort Sumner down the Pecos 150 miles almost to the Texas line.

But that was still to come, and when we reached our destination with the big herd, I said to 'Uncle John', 'What now?'

'Now,' he grinned, 'I build myself the biggest ranch house ever seen in these parts. Ain't it strange, Charlie? Nearly all this valley belongs to me.'

'To you?'

'Yes, the whole caboodle.'

'But, this is free range.'

'It was. It ain't no more. You're standing on my land, Goodnight, and don't you forget it.'

'But, how come?'

'What do you mean, how come? I've claimed it, ain't I?'

'You have?' I must have sounded very dim to him. 'How did you do that?'

Chisum reached in his back pocket and pulled out a copy of the *Las Vegas Times*. He pointed to an advertisement on the front page. 'I, John Chisum, hereby state that I have taken possessory rights of the land on the Pecos Plain running from old Fort Sumner to . . . '

'Is that all you have to do?'

'Well, it ain't all you have to do. It helps if you go see the territorial governor and, you know' — he rubbed thumb and forefinger together — 'grease a few palms. And then have your rights all drawn up legal like.'

'That's what you've done?'

'Of course.'

'Hmm, that's a pity, because I was thinking I wouldn't mind having some of this land, myself.'

'You're a bit slow off the mark, Charlie. But there's some land down the south end, a bit rocky, not very good grass. I'd be glad to have you as a neighbour. You did a fine job blazing this trail.'

'You don't say? A fine idiot I am, too.'

'You've been paid well, aincha, Charlie? What you whingeing at? Go north. There's plenty more land to be had. Claim your homesteader's two hundred acres and push out from

188

there. But don't shilly-shally. There's a flood of people looking for land. And when you get hold of it, hang on to it' — he slapped the Colt on his thigh — 'with a gun, if need be. That's the only law in this land. My boys have got orders to run off any trespassers. They're a hard bunch, but they're the sort you need. Don't worry, you'll always be welcome to call, or take your cattle through. Don't get any ideas of treading on my toes, that's all.'

'Whew!' I gave a whistle. 'You've certainly taught me a thing or two, Mr Chisum. I'm gonna have to smarten myself up.'

14

It was true. Colorado was God's own country. A land of majestic mountains rising to 15,000 feet, their sides swathed by dark pine forests, and scarred by deep wooded canyons, opening onto fine pastures. To a man used to Texan plains it was an awesome sight. And here a man had to learn to live on terms with brown bears and grizzly, mountain lions, wolves, wild cats, beavers, minks, elks, eagles, rattlesnakes and skunks of both the two-legged and four-legged variety. For wherever gold is found townships full of shifty ne'er-do-wells abound, *and* their female camp followers.

We rode north, my two *amigos* and I, on our sturdy mustangs, and I guess we looked a colourful trio, a tall Texan, a little bald-headed Mexican, and a happy-go-lucky coloured boy, in our range clothes. We took a look at the country and decided that the southernmost part of the state, west of Pueblo, along the Arkansas River, was the best land for cattle rearing.

By this time I had amassed some $70,000 by droving beeves so I started buying up choice stretches of land along the river, remembering the maxim that he who has the rights to water for his cattle is king. Soon I had strategic pastures along twenty-five miles of river and, in the manner of Chisum, had claimed possessory right of the intervening lands back as far as the foothills. I had a cabin bunkhouse built and hired a couple of men who knew how to use guns to guard the property in my absence. Then Jesus, Moses and myself set off on the thousand-mile ride south to raise another longhorn herd.

John Wesley Iliffe was by now the biggest cattle baron in Colorado. It was his proud boast that he could ride for seven days across his ranches on the South Platte River and stay

191

at a different ranch house of his own every night. That, to me, seemed a reasonable ambition.

But raising cattle was a different kettle of fish in these northern climes. There were bitter, blizzard-bound winters to nurse the beeves through. The longhorns were hardy enough. From yearlings, I left them for three years to roam as wild as buffalo until they were a good 900 pounds and ready for sale as beef to the miners, Indian agencies, or the workers on the Union Pacific railroad. Or, otherwise, herded them up to Cheyenne for shipment on the railroad to Chicago, and the meat-hungry East.

I had started breeding high-grade shorthorn Durhams, however, to try to improve texture and weight of the beef, and they were more delicate li'l darlin's. The experiment did not really pay off. We had to spend a lot of time cutting and storing hay to feed them in the winters, and even bring them into covered huts during the worst of the snows when the mercury fell into the waybelows. All those cows needed were bedside reading lamps we mollycoddled them so much!

But, I was making money. I had the men dig ditches to irrigate the land, plant orchards, grow vegetables, and start work on a big two-storey ranch house. All I needed was someone to share it with me during the long lonesome winters. I had become one of the most prosperous ranchers in Colorado, but my life hadn't changed a lot. I still spent most days in the saddle, riding the bounds, tending the herd, protecting it from men who thought they might help themselves to my stock, and seeing off immigrants who had ideas of moving onto my lands. 'Once you let a mouse start nibbling at the edges of your cheese then pretty soon you ain't got much left,' I was at pains to explain to them as I sat my horse, my Spencer propped on one knee. They generally agreed this made sense and moved on.

By now Colorado had become something of a magnet for asthmatics and consumptives, a veritable convention of 'em arrived to take the mountain camp cure. And there were a few tourists, too, coming out by railroad to Cheyenne and heading on horseback south to see the wonders of the mountain scenery. Mostly, I sent them packing, too.

But one morning I was surprised to see riding side-saddle towards me across the snowy wastes a young lady, wrapped in a fur-lined shawl, and kinda top-heavy in a huge feathered hat. She was accompanied by a disreputable character known as Mountain Jim, who, with long hair to his shoulders, and in ragged buckskins, claimed to be her guide. His usual habitat was saloons, and he was renowned as a foul-mouthed trouble-maker and killer when in his cups.

The girl's eyes had a somewhat frightened and luminous glow to them, her soft flaxen hair streaked by the fierce

194

wind across her face, and she seemed somewhat breathless and distressed.

'What'n hell you doin' this far out?' I said, somewhat gruffly, I guess, because I was getting tired of interlopers on my land. And a no-good like Jim and some snooty gal from the East were the last ones I wanted.

'I'm showing the young leddy the sights,' he crackled, and leaning back in the saddle swept a finger towards the distant icy-fanged mountains. 'Thar y'ar, I tol' ya. Ya git a fine view of Pike's Peak. See, over yonder.'

'Yes,' she murmured, and gave me a faint smile. 'I'm dreadfully cold and tired. We've been camping out. I don't suppose there's any chance around here of refreshments?'

I pursed my lips and studied her, quizzically. And it was as if I read something in her eyes. It was as if I suddenly knew that she was the one who had been sent to me.

'Follow me, miss,' I said, and, as she passed me, pushed Paddy forward to block Mountain Jim's way. 'Not you. You can git back to them scum you generally hang out with. I'll see she gets back to Denver or wherever she has to go.'

'What you talkin' about?' — his hand instinctively went to the butt of his revolver but mine did, too. 'I ain't been paid yet. She owes me twenty dollars. Those were the terms.'

I dug in my jacket and flipped him a golden eagle. 'Just hand over her luggage. And then git off my land.'

He scowled, untied a carpet bag from his jackpack, tossed it to me. 'Think you're high and mighty, doncha?' He wheeled his animals and turned back the way he had come. 'You'll see,' he called back. 'One of these days . . . ' His words spluttered out on the wind in curses. I kneed my bronc towards him and he set off at a run. But the next year Mountain Jim was shot dead by a settler.

The girl, huddled in her shawl, had

been watching all this with a curious expression.

'I took the liberty of dismissing your guide,' I said. 'Come on.'

I took her into my big new ranch house and sat her down in front of the log fire, made her a coffee in the kitchen, and watched her freckled cheeks glow as she thawed out. 'Thank goodness that dreadful man's gone,' she said, giving me a smile. 'It's been a nightmare. His cursing, his staggering about around the campfire. I told him I would go on my own, but he wouldn't let me. It's nice to meet someone not stinking of whiskey.'

'Might I ask you your name, miss?'

'Mary Ann.'

'Mary Ann!' I shouted with alarm.

'What's wrong?'

'No, nuthin'! It's jest that I once knew a Mary Ann. But she was like a durn wild mustang, whereas you strike me as being a thoroughbred.'

'So, why don't you call me Molly. My family do.'

197

'Molly. Yeah, that's more homely. I like it. I'm Charlie.'

'It's very nice here, Charlie. Perhaps you should introduce me to your employer? I wonder if he could provide me with accommodation for a day or two. Is he home?'

'Oh, he's home, all right. Guess you figure me for a 'puncher. Well, to tell the truth, I never did cotton on to having someone boss me about. I kinda own this outfit.'

'You do? Are you Mr Goodnight?'

'That's me.'

'How odd,' she smiled, staring at me in my range clothes. 'I mean, how rude of me. I do apologize.'

It turned out she was from an aristocratic old family in Kentucky, and, against their wishes, was doing a 'grand tour' of America before settling down. 'Though I'm not sure I'll ever settle down,' she smiled.

'You don't, don't ya? Waal, maybe you got another think coming.'

'Really? Why?'

'Because I'm gonna marry ya.' I took a thick silver Navajo ring from my little finger, and placed it on hers. 'That's if you'll have me.'

'Well,' she said, blinking with surprise. 'You certainly know how to sweep a gal off her feet.'

'I been waiting a long time,' I said.

As chance had it a blizzard set in and we were snowed up for a week. And when the sun shone again on an ocean of ice outside I went for a preacher and we got wed the next day. I guess the telegraph to Molly's folks came as a bit of a surprise.

* * *

We didn't go on honeymoon because I was too busy out with the men trying to rescue beeves which had got buried in snowdrifts. I liked to have men around me whom I could trust, who knew cattle, and I employed them on a permanent basis, not just for the summer like other ranchers.

I had made Jesus the ramrod, which sometimes jarred, him being Mex, but they soon saw his mettle.

'You figure you done the right thing, getting hitched, Charlie?' he asked me.

'Yes, I do. Oliver Loving was right. She's damn wonderful.'

And, she was. It was great to have her waiting for me every night. And, although she'd never been brought up to it, Molly proved a fine housekeeper. She also busied herself doing my paperwork. Of course, she missed some of the comforts of civilization, books, and theatres, and fashions and suchlike, but I tried to make it up to her by importing wagon-loads of knick-knacks for the house, fine china, curtains, feather beds, wine coolers, even a billiard table and piano, anything, in fact, that money could buy to keep us amused during the long winter evenings.

In the summer we took a delayed honeymoon travelling on the newly completed railroad from Cheyenne across The Rockies, climbing to the giddy heights of Cape Horn, and down to Sacramento and San Francisco in all the luxury of our own Pullman sleeper. It was interesting to see the sea, and the tall sailing ships in the harbour, and the cable car and opera, and all those folks, but we were both glad to get back to our ranch house. We were happiest when we had time to go off on horseback up into the mountains, to hunt for our food, and camp out by clear pools, and see the glorious sunsets and the reflected afterglow colouring the sheer mountain cliffsides.

One evening we were having dinner in the house when Jesus clattered in, somewhat excited. 'We got trouble,' he said to me in a low voice. 'Cattle run off. We figure it the Coe gang.'

'What's wrong?' Molly called.

'Nothing,' I said, taking a carbine from the rack. 'I gotta go out, thassall.' Sixty masked vigilantes were waiting for me down by the corral . . .

Four hours later I returned as she

was preparing for bed. 'Everything's OK,' I told her.

Three days later at breakfast, she was reading *The Rocky Mountain News* and remarked, sharply, 'It says here two men were found hanging from a telegraph pole adjacent to the Goodnight ranch — '

'Waal,' I drawled, drinking my coffee. 'I don't suppose it hurt the telegraph pole none.'

'Charlie.' Her eyes were startled as they met mine across the top of the paper. 'Are you saying — '

'It's a different way of life out here, Molly. A man has to make his own law. Am I supposed to let them steal my cows?'

She frowned, her eyes hardening, did not say any more, and went to her room. I knew she did not like it, but we never spoke about it again.

Influenced by England's Queen Victoria, even in Colorado high standards of morality and etiquette prevailed. Molly, a devout churchgoer, was very fond of riding but always felt nervous side-saddle. Ladies were not supposed to ride astride. To open their legs on horseback was considered indelicate. So I made her a special saddle with a hooked extension of padded leather she could fit her knee in beneath her long skirt and ride all snug and secure. Again I forgot to patent it and pretty soon, to my chagrin, I saw the Denver Ladies Saddle advertised in a mail-order magazine. In time it became pretty popular throughout the land. Molly certainly looked the perfect lady using it. Queen Victoria would have been proud of her!

By 1873 I had become one of the richest cattlemen in Colorado. But there were no free cattle any more and I had to invest money to restock my vast range. To do this I had become a heavy user of credit. The high interest charged, as much as two per cent a month, annoyed me, as it did other ranchers. We decided to beat the bankers by opening our own. So we formed an organization we called the Pueblo Stock Growers Bank.

It was just our luck we opened the same month as the Great Crash that crippled the country. I found myself practically wiped off the face of the earth. Against Molly's advice I tried to recover my losses by buying more stock. Prices sank to rock bottom. I lost all my money and most of my cows. I was finally left with about $100 in my pocket, the amount I had seven years before when I first met Jesus Gerrigueta de Peyera in that Freedom cantina and decided to go seriously into the cattle business.

It was gloomy selling the land and stock to pay my creditors. By the time it was over I was left with about 1,800 cows. We sat on a box and watched the bailiffs strip the house, the piano, the pictures; everything had to go.

'Waal, gal,' I said, squeezing her hand. 'One day you're up, and the next you're down. I'm certainly not going to be able to keep you in the manner you're accustomed to. Maybe it might be an idea if you went back to your family for a bit while I try to sort things out.'

I didn't want to, but I was giving her the chance to leave. Many a woman would have done.

'Don't be a fool,' she said, kissing my cheek. 'Didn't you hear me say 'for better or worse, richer or poorer'? I'll never leave you. Why don't I hang on here, look after what cattle's left, while you — '

'What, start again? What with? Where? All the land's been taken.'

'Didn't I hear you say that there was still an area of Texas where no man had settled? That the migration routes, the trails swept around it?'

'The Staked Plains? The Panhandle? The Llanos Estacados? Only Comanches ever lived there. You any idea what that land's like? It's so dry the early explorers called it the Sahara of America. It's a great, flat, treeless expanse cut through with canyons and gullies. No white man in his right mind would want to try and ranch there.'

'Well, you say yourself you're crazy, Charlie.'

'Not that crazy.'

'If it's grassland you can run cattle on it. Why don't you go take a look?'

'Poor grassland. You'd need fifteen acres for each cow. It's so lonesome out there, only the whine of the wind, and coyotes and Comanches for company; it's no place for you, gal.'

'I'll wait for you, Charlie. You send for me when you're ready.'

'What about all your church friends in Pueblo? You didn't like me riding with the vigilantes here, Molly. You would hate it a durn sight more out there. You'd have to learn to use a gun, yourself. To shoot to kill. Don't think it would be easy. There's Comanches still on the prowl. And plenty of white bad hats, too.'

'I'll take lessons in shooting while you're away,' she laughed. 'Charlie, you may think me a helpless woman, but don't worry, I know the score. And where you go, I go.'

15

We had searched the windswept wastes of the Llanos Estacados for two summers looking for a rumoured deep canyon, well watered, which might still be the haunt of Comanche and *comanchero*, but could well be transformed into a cattleman's Eden. I was beginning to think it must be nothing more than a fable, that this search would never end. The Staked Plains had not yet been properly explored or mapped and, in spite of being hit hard by Nelson Miles's military, many Comanche had refused to go into the reservations and were still lord of the plains. We knew that going into that area was a dangerous thing to do.

Consequently, I had enrolled three men who knew how to fight, masterly with rope, knife or gun, Leigh Dyer,

Dave McCormick and John Rumans, and my two *compadres*, Jesus and Moses. I had furnished them with the '73, that year's carbine brought out by Oliver Winchester, a twelve-shot repeater, and plenty of bullets.

We would need them if we were to run into Indians. One of the most feared Comanche chiefs at large was Quanah Parker, none other than the blue-eyed, half-breed son of Cynthia Ann Parker. Word was he had mustered a war party of 700 warriors, Cheyenne, Kiowa, Arapaho, and his own Qwahadi braves. The odds for us would not be good if we ran into them.

'Riders coming!' Moses hollered one afternoon, charging back to us.

'Hold steady, son,' I said, but like every man my hand had instantly gone to my six-shooter. I peered across the ragged land with its harsh ditches and escarpments, the silvery-blue tableland, and my initial relief was to see there were only about twenty of them. There was a glint of sunshine on silver pommels and bridles and I tensed.

'Look like *comancheros*,' I said, my hand going to the sheath of my own fifteen-shot Winchester rifle. I pulled it out and levered in the new centre-fire cartridge loaded with a .44 calibre bullet and forty grains of powder. This gave the weapon a considerable increase in range and stopping power over the earlier model. The leading Mexican was getting closer, riding straight towards us. I tucked the rifle into my shoulder and sighted on him.

'He ain't gonna know what's hit him.'

Jesus glanced across at me, anxiously. 'Thirty of them to six of us. It ain't good odds, Charlie.'

'With this it is,' I gritted out.

'Hold on. I go forward, talk to them. You cover me.'

I watched him ride forward, and parlay, ready any moment to see him cut down. But, no, Jesus returned, riding beside the leader at the head of them. They were a harsh-looking bunch, in tight velveteens and wide-brimmed sombreros, riding spirited mustangs with ornate harness and stirrups covered by *tapaderos*.

'Iss OK,' Jesus called. 'I know this bunch. They *mesteneros*. They out looking for wild horses.'

'Yeah?' I said, keeping my rifle in my hand. 'Is that what they say?'

'*Si, señor.*' Jesus gave me a wink. 'They know this land like back of hand. Maybe they can help us.'

I asked them to step down, join us for a powwow, a smoke and coffee. They did so, and one of them, an old man with a thin face rutted with lines and a grey stubble, listened attentively, as Jesus described the place we were seeking.

'I know that place,' the old man, Martinez, cried out. 'For many years I was a *comanchero* until a year or two ago the soldiers disrupted our business. A vast wild gorge. We used to meet Lone Wolf's Comanches there.'

'You did? Well, maybe you can lead us there?'

'I could,' he smiled, toothlessly. 'For a price.'

'I'll pay you ten dollars a day to be my guide,' I said.

He told the others and they laughed, said they would be drifting on their way, he could catch them up.

* * *

For three days we wandered behind this character until I began to wonder if he was simply taking my money and thought me a fool Texan. He led us for miles, zig-zagging back and forth.

When he reached a ravine he would frown. 'No, this not it.' When nightfall came he would slap his head and say, 'I no understand. This crazy. Perhaps it get washed away?'

'How could it get washed away? You said it was wide enough to build a city in. I'll give you one more day. And then' — I snapped my fingers — 'Pouf!'

212

Maybe he needed a little fear putting into him.

To tell the truth, I was beginning to give up hope. The Llanos Estacados was a harsh and inhospitable place. The plains between the ravines were stove-lid flat and boundless, a parched surface empty of all but grey soil and dry grass. The next day the old Mexican led us up a steep ridge out of which the silvery clouds seemed to billow. Suddenly we were on the edge of a mighty chasm.

'*Por fin!*' Martinez cried, as we looked down into a great gorge with walls 1,000 feet deep. 'At last, *señor*.'

'Jeez!' I whispered, peeling off forty dollars to pay him. 'So, it's really true.'

At this upper western end the canyon was narrow and lined with cedars and wild china. Awed, we rode on along its rim and noted it widen to form a vast cattleman's heaven, watered by what must have been a headwater of the Red River, and sheltered and fenced by its own towering bluffs.

I sat my paint and stared down. 'This is going to be mine,' I hissed out. 'You all hear me? I'm laying claim to it. I'm taking it by any means necessary, legal, illegal or extra-legal. I'll drive out the buffalo and bring in my own herds. And if the Comanch', or anybody else, want to argue, they'll have to answer to my guns.'

* * *

We carefully marked and mapped the trail so we wouldn't lose this Eden again. And we rode back to Pueblo to collect Molly and the remains of my herd. She was, naturally, overjoyed to hear the news. We had some good friends in Pueblo because, when I had funds, I had sponsored the building of a church and school, and they had looked after her. We said our goodbyes and set off back on the trail across the great plains.

On the way we fell in with two young

adventurers, a Scot, J C Johnston, and a rather haughty public-school Englishman, James Hughes, whose father had written a book called *Tom Brown's Schooldays*. They asked if they could join us and, being sorely in need of hard cash, I let them invest in a third interest in the herd. I guessed I'd have to put up with their weird foppish ways.

When we reached the fabulous canyon, which we called the Palo Duro, we moved the cattle down single-file on an old Indian trail. It was a tricky business descending hundreds of feet to the bottom which was swathed in lush buffalo grass, but we didn't lose any.

'No way we gonna get the chuck wagon down,' Jesus said.

'There is a way. We dismantle it and lower it on lariats,' I said. 'There's always a way if you look for it.'

Along the stream there were cedars and willows, and it was strangely peacefully shielded from the constant prairie wind. 'It's beautiful,' Molly cried, hugging me. 'Charlie, it's really beautiful.'

'It's not only that, it's ideal,' I grunted. 'Where else on this continent could you find a finer natural location? See this stretch of level grassland? This is where we're gonna build our home. And we ain't never leaving. Nobody's gonna put us out this time. I promise you that, Molly.'

There were tears in her eyes as she hugged me again. 'You old scoundrel. I love you.'

'And me you,' I muttered, for I was never one to show my emotions, not with the boys watching.

★ ★ ★

The first job was to clear the canyon of bison. Yelling and whip cracking we soon had a great herd of 10,000 of them, a sea of brown, hump-backed beasts, thundering away down the mighty canyon, firing bullets at the feet of the laggards, while hundreds of little black bears went scuttling away in fright up among the ledges of the rimrock. After that, driving out buffalo was a regular duty of my herders for two or three years until the scourge of the buffalo hunters meant that very few remained.

The next job was to start work on the house, the men's bunkhouse and the corrals, to fortify them with shutters and gunports to deter any attack by Comanches. We had no need to build fences; the canyon walls acted as a natural barrier. Even if the cattle grazed high up on its slopes they could not climb over the sheer caprock rim.

On looking around I realized that the canyon slashed the Llanos in two, and how anybody had not discovered and settled it before was a mystery. It seemed like it had been waiting for me. I looked at the Navajo bracelet on my wrist. Maybe it really had magic properties?

★ ★ ★

When we had gotten organized and there didn't seem to be any immediate threat from Quanah Parker — he had been busy attacking buffalo hunters, his pet hate, at Adobe Walls — we went off to raise more stock in Denver.

An odd thing happened on that journey. I met a man who was to play a large part in my life, John Adair, a wealthy Irishman, whose wife was the former Cornelia Wadsworth, of the Newport and New York social register. They were highflyers, in love with the West in a romantically notioned way, not really my kind of people. But they were very impressed by my story. And, it was becoming apparent, to go big in cattle a man needed a backer. They were holding a high-faluting shindig in a Denver hotel. We were invited, and during the evening they made me an offer I found difficult to refuse.

'Charlie,' Molly said, anxiously. 'I don't like this. It sounds like you're planning to sell out to them.'

'I ain't gonna sell out, gal,' I said, in a lowered voice. 'These two sweethearts are fish who I'm gonna hook. We'll take 'em back to the ranch, let 'em play cowboys for a bit, and throw 'em a line. I'm looking for a big bite. Adair's told me he's got half-a-million dollars to invest.'

She studied me with those severe grey eyes of hers. 'I hope you know what you're doing.'

'I only had elementary schoolin', gal, but I've learned a few tricks along the way. Them lawyers of their's ain't gonna outfox me.'

The debonair and talkative John Adair was keen to take a look at our land, so we set off back, driving a herd of 100 shorthorn bulls, Molly at the reins of the wagon, and the Adairs riding alongside. Cornelia, his wife, was the daughter of a New York banking tycoon and sister of a senator. She rode side-saddle, dressed in the height of fashion, highly animated in conversation, and a tad crazy, no doubt due to being spoiled rotten. Nonetheless, she and my plain-spoken Molly got on well.

In fact, when we got back to the Palo Duro we all had a fine old time. I led them out at a gallop across the plains chasing a pack of wolves who had been ham-stringing and dining off my herd, shooting them from horseback, and they voted it better than fox-hunting. They were highly excited when we came upon a herd of buffalo and chased them down to take trophies. The bracing air gave them keen appetites, and I guess eating plain food, prairie grouse and buffalo hump they had shot themselves, gave it an edge on the stuffy and pampered existence of a New York mansion. I hammed up the role of the trusty Western frontiersman, the legend I seemed to have become, and they lapped it up, keeping us jawing and drinking into the early hours. I was very keen to expand my herd enormously across all the available land at my disposal, and told Adair that if I did so I could double my outlay in the time it took a yearling to mature to prime beef. I laid it on with a trowel, but it was basically the truth. All I needed was the cash to invest, and, grudgingly, I allowed them to persuade me to let them be partners.

'Look,' I said, 'let's just make out a straightforward agreement. Out here in the West we don't take kindly to lawyers and all their addendums and double-talk, their *mutatis mutandis* and gobbledegook. Let's sit down right now and work it out.'

And that we did. I agreed to purchase more land, develop and manage the ranch in their absence and stock it with cattle and horses through money furnished by Adair. For this I was to receive $25,000 a year salary. At the end of five years I was to acquire one third of the land, cattle and horses, out of which I would pay back Adair one third of the money invested.

'Charlie, this is wonderful,' Cornelia gushed, as we signed the contract, and she immediately began making plans for building a big stone residence not far from us. 'We could have our own stables and blacksmiths shop and a mess hall for the men nearby.'

'Have what you like,' I said magnanimously, seeing as they would be paying. 'You can have your own tin shop for making plates and cups.'

'Oh, no,' she trilled. 'We'll import silverware from New York.'

'We will be needing more staff,' Adair said. 'I suggest further down the valley we build a small township of, say, fifty houses, where they can live. We should bring in skilled tradesmen and their families, who can supply our needs.'

'Why not?' I croaked, although I was beginning to think this thing was getting out of hand. 'We could do that.'

They were in seventh heaven pacing out the land, and drawing up designs for their home, so, just to show I was taking them seriously, I set some of the boys to hauling great rocks with the wagon oxen to make a start on the foundations.

'It's certainly going to be different to our place,' I muttered to Molly, for we'd built ourselves a simple two-up, two-down, log and plank cabin. And fortified it with a ditch and stockade. 'Still, just as long as they feel at home.'

Fortunately, while they were with us we didn't get no blizzards, prairie fires, locust storms, or visits from Comanche, which might have deterred them. They set off promising to have the cash forthcoming and to see us the following summer.

And I set about purchasing 24,000 acres of public land at seventy-five cents an acre, which wasn't a great amount, but I chose it in crazy quilted spots with access to the water, so that I could effectively take further 'possessory rights' to all the land lying back within fifteen or twenty-five miles of the water. So, effectively, this gave me control of the whole of the Palo Duro canyon. John Chisum had taught me well!

If anybody wanted to argue, well, I had hired boys who carried guns and weren't afraid to use them. In the final analysis there can be no free land claimed without the backing of a six-gun. It wasn't just me; it was the way it happened from Montana to Arizona. The gun was law.

The Adairs were as good as their word. Their cash duly arrived in my bank account. So, I guess I must have blazed another trail for I was the first cattleman to bring in foreign backing which in later years became commonplace, many ranchers being forced to sell out to Scottish and English investors. I figure we made the first and the best deal.

For my part, I honoured my bargain. I used my expertise in cattle to build up the herds, and used $150,000 of the

Adairs' to bring in more blooded bulls — 2,000 of them. I had to hire more hands for there was one hell of a lot of work to do in riding the bounds and keeping the cattle healthy. Soon came the summer round-up and branding. The Adairs wired to say they were going to Monte Carlo and, to tell the truth, I breathed a sigh of relief.

In the winter I put some manpower to blasting rocks from the cliffsides, hauling them to the spot by the river the Adairs had chosen, and building their mansion. I had planed planks made and polished so they could have floorboards, and brought in carpenters to craft the banisters and fol-de-rols. When they visited the next summer it would be finished.

Barns, corrals, bunkhouses, blacksmith's and dairy went up apace. When you have the money and the labour you can do anything! And a start was made on building the new village which eventually would number some fifty houses. Everything was getting a tad too civilized for my taste, but I had agreed it should be done, so I did it.

Molly had taken to raising chickens for eggs, but she never would allow them to be killed, and mollycoddled them and chattered to them like pets. She planned to get milk for our coffee and make butter and cheese, but milking an ornery wild range cow is no easy matter. I had to appoint one of the boys to rope these cows twice a day when she wanted to milk them, drive them into the corral, snub their heads close to the post, and tie their hind legs together so they wouldn't kick the pail over as Molly sat on her stool! It sure was nice, though, to have half-a-dozen fresh fried eggs, butter on my sourdough biscuits, and cream in my coffee for breakfast.

By the end of the following summer I decided to send a big part of the herd north, mainly grown longhorn steers, to sell. 'There ain't no need for me to come,' I told John Rumens. 'I'm making you trail boss.'

He looked a trifle startled. 'How do I find the way to Cheyenne?'

'Hell,' I growled. 'Just keep your eye on the north star and keep 'em moving 'til you hit the railroad.'

The reason I didn't want to go was that there had been a lot of Indian activity building up. Further north, beyond the railroad, it was rumoured that 20,000 Sioux and Cheyenne were mustering ready for war. They objected to goldseekers entering their sacred Black Hills.

Here in the Panhandle the Comanche were again causing us trouble. Many had deserted the reservations to ride out and take up arms with Quanah Parker's renegades. The incursions of ranchers and settlers like myself seemed to have spurred them to one frenzied last stand. A cloud of smoke on the horizon generally warned us we would find the burned-out wagon of some emigrant or mule-skinner, and scalped and mutilated bodies on the ground.

On one occasion they set fire to a

mile-long stretch of grass. 'What we gonna do, boss?' Moses yelled. 'We got no water to put it out.' Prairie fire could put fear into a man worse than stampede.

'Shoot two steers,' I hollered.

'What for?'

'You'll see.' It was an experiment of mine, but it worked. We dragged the bloody and damp carcasses back and forth, galloping the terrified horses along close to the blaze so they were in dire danger of their hooves getting burned by the cinders. But, it worked. The blaze finally smouldered out.

'Lousy redskins,' I muttered, peering through the smoky haze towards the empty horizon. I had the feeling they were watching us.

When we returned to the valley I ordered everybody at work on the new building to camp out in the corrals and barns alongside the house. They would, I hoped, be safer in this stockaded cantonment around the house. Behind and at the sides of us was the protection of the sheer walls. They could only come in from the open valley. I set guards on the cliffs to watch.

'Whass matter, Charlie?' Jesus asked, as he came, in his poncho and sombrero, to lean on the corral fence with me and gaze up at the stars. 'You edgy tonight?'

'It's jest a feelin' I allus git at the back of my neck when them varmints around — the hair kinda prickles like a dog's.'

He laughed, but checked the carbine under his arm and, together, we rode out and up the cliffsides to speak to the boys, but all was uncannily quiet. One said he thought he had seen what might be a campfire light out on the plain, but couldn't be sure of it.

* * *

It was early dawn when they hit. Moses came charging in on his mustang along the riverbank, hollering at the top of his lungs, his hat fanned back by the breeze, quirting his mount from side to side as he came splashing through the shallows. 'Comanche!' he screamed as we opened up the gate to let him through.

That was more than apparent as we heard their spine-chilling, high-pitched screaming. Comanche. Hundreds of them. A galloping wall of tossing eagle feathers, brandishing weapons, dark, lithe figures on painted horses, coming at speed towards us, their bullets and arrows already hissing about us. And one of our carpenters gave an answering scream as a flint-tipped, greasewood shaft pierced his abdomen and he fell back, writhing.

Molly had run to kneel beside him, but I shouted at her, 'Get back in the house. He's finished.' She stared at the poor man's face, and then at me, and her eyes were as hard as that time they found the two men hanging. But she did as I bid and backed away to the house, her face distraught. 'Get your

gun ready. And be prepared to use it,'
I yelled.

I turned back to feed slugs into my
Winchester and fired rapidly into the
oncoming wave of warriors. I had the
gratification of seeing two I had aimed
at dislodged from horseback and go
spinning across the grass to lie still.
But the wave came thundering on until
it smashed against our stockade wall in
a turmoil of screaming, writhing horses
and bloodied warriors.

We had built the stockade well,
with a ditch and stout sharpened logs
pointed out at them at a 45° angle.
And it stopped them. They were unable
to leap their horses across, or make a
manual assault with any ease, although
two or three did, hauling themselves
over, poised with painted faces, and
jumping down upon us. One tumbled
the Scot, Johnston, over, and had his
scalping knife raised, but his friend,
Hughes, threw a rugby tackle and
hauled him away. He grappled for the
knife as the Scot recovered and shot

the Indian in the head, splattering his friend with blood.

The first wave retreated, but I could see it was not going to be the last. There must have been about 700 of the savages milling about the valley and the riverbanks, and I could see from their body paint that they were mainly Qwahadi, the fiercest of all Comanche tribes. Some were proudly adorned in eagle feather headdresses trailing behind them, others were bareheaded, their long hair flailing out, and some wore peculiar little pillboxes like baskets. Some wore fringed buckskins, but others were nearly as naked as nature intended, in just a rag of loincloth and moccasins. To me, their faces were as dark and ugly as sin. Some carried stolen army carbines, with which they haphazardly peppered us, others lances, or bows, with quivers of arrows on their backs, with which they could reload almost as quickly as a revolver could fire. And be just as deadly and accurate.

A second charge had come screaming in, and we had managed to repulse that, too. But some of the attackers had climbed up around the stockade on the cliffsides and were raining their arrows and bullets down on us. The air was thick with gunsmoke, rolling in clouds, and as more and more Indians leapt down upon us, we were hard pressed in hand-to-hand combat. Knives flashed, revolvers crashed, a skull crasher smashed into the head of a 'puncher spilling out his brains.

The horsemen outside were retreating to reform, and I saw a tall Comanche, lithely muscled, but featherless, his plaits sheathed in otter fur, sitting a restless mustang, directing operations with his carbine. I had an idea he must be Quanah Parker, and snapped off a shot from my Remington at him, but his horse leapt away as I did so.

Already five of our men were lying dead or wounded on the ground. 'Get back in the house,' I shouted. 'There's too many of 'em to hold.'

233

The twenty-five men left did so, dragging the wounded with us, crowding into the house and bolting the door. We hurriedly took up positions at the gunports in the shutters. I ran upstairs and found Molly at our shuttered bedroom window. She had her Winchester tucked in her shoulder and was firing like a demon. She wiped her hair from her eyes when she saw me, and gave me a brief, guilty smile. 'I've killed at least three, God help me.'

'It's them or us, gal,' I said, knowing I would have to save my last bullet to kill her rather than let her fall into their hands. 'There's wounded downstairs. Can you help them? I'll take over here.'

She went to do as I suggested, doing the best she could for the injured, and reloading rifles for the defenders at the ports. Meanwhile, the battle raged on for two or more hours. We held them off with our long-range rifles, their carbines and arrows having little effect on our thick log walls.

Many of the Comanche had dismounted and were sneaking up out of our angle of fire to try to get at us. There was the thudding of axes at the front door, so I opened my shutter and leaned out and put a stop to that. And then there was a scraping and slithering on the roof. Somehow one had managed to get up there. I waited until I heard his footfall and fired through the shingles. He screamed and tumbled away.

Others had run forward with blazing brands in their hands to hurl at the roof and walls. 'I say, that isn't cricket!' Hughes cried out, joining me at the open window and, with a rifle shot, tumbled one of the fire-bearers in his tracks. 'Bastards, aren't they?'

'You can say that again,' I grinned through his smoke. 'I think they're having second thoughts. They're losing too many men.'

By now the gates had been broken in and the tall Indian galloped up fearlessly towards us, his plaits flying in the wind. He looked up at me and I saw the gleam of his vivid blue eyes in his harsh-cut dark face, as he hurled his lance. It nearly parted my hair.

I kneeled back and had him in my sights. I could have ploughed a bullet through his chest. And young Hughes was about to do the same. But, I held out a hand restraining him. For some reason, maybe because I was thinking of Cynthia Ann, his mother, I was reluctant to kill him. He had turned and was trotting his horse away. 'Let him go.'

We watched as Quanah Parker began calling off his men. 'Hold your fire,' I shouted. 'Let them take their wounded.'

They did so, melting away, back towards the prairie, taking some of our mustangs. I knew it was the last time we would see them.

* * *

After that, I guess the Comanche realized it was no use going on fighting. Quanah Parker led his men in to surrender. He was greatly respected by us Texans and he turned into a major motivator of peace terms for his nation. He settled in Indian Territory, became a successful farmer, a friend of President Roosevelt, and a judge. I often thought it a shame his mother hadn't lived. She would have been proud of him.

By then, five years from starting, I ruled the Palo Duro and all the outlying plains further than a man could see. I presided over a herd that numbered over 100,000 head, from which I sold 30,000 animals in an average season for a gross income of around half-a-million dollars. At least Molly seemed to be mightily pleased. Her only complaint was loneliness when I was away. 'Go and see your neighbour,' I told her. 'Old Tom Bugbee. He's only fifty miles away!'

She had more company than she

bargained for when John Adair died prematurely. His widow kept on the partnership and descended on us with a posse of guests of some social magnificence, wagonloads of personal baggage, a battalion of maids, butlers and secretaries, and crates of champagne, which she swilled at her hoedowns until the early hours. Fortunately her visits were not that frequent. She certainly gave the folks in these parts something to talk about.

I tried to reign over my 'fiefdom' as some called it, as fairly as possible. In fact, when some people of Mexican blood took to running small sheep herds on the edges of my land other ranchers were keen for me to lead them in reprisals against them and their animals. In other words, shoot them all, as had happened in other parts of the country. I was by no means convinced that sheep poisoned the water or ruined the grass, and saw no reason why we couldn't co-exist. So, in no uncertain terms, I told them to leave them be. And, it so happened, my word was law. They went off with their tails between their legs.

Jesus slapped me on the back and grinned, 'You're a good man, Charlie.'

That, I guess, was more reward than all the money: to be thought well of. So, when a colony of Methodists set to farming in the district and the cowboys contemptuously harassed their 'Saints Roost', I told them to cut it out. And they did.

One thing did bother me. I had spent a lot of time experimenting to improve my herd and had brought in white-face Herefords. These highgrade cattle it turned out were susceptible to the Texas cattle tick. Longhorns themselves were immune. I was sadly forced to issue an ultimatum that if any rancher tried to trail herds of rough longhorns, without doubt carrying Texas fever, across my lands they would be stopped.

'I do not wish to hurt men,' I wrote in a letter to one of these ranchers, 'but

239

I simply say that you will never cross my lands in good health.'

What did hurt *me* was that he chose to publish this in the *Texas Echo* and I was denounced as some kind of overbearing tyrant.

Nonetheless, I kept my gun handy.

Well, I guess that just about tells my story. I've got to get on with my latest experiment. I'm trying to breed a cow with a buffalo. It ought to be the perfect animal. However, my first hybrid has turned out with a buffalo hump, a goat-like beard, and a voice like a low-pitched pig grunt. I've got a feeling it might be nothing but a big mistake!

Sometimes, when I drive Molly fifteen miles to the Methodist church, and prop my rifle in the aisle against our pew — just in case the Comanche take it in their heads to come back — as the preacher man drones on I get to dreaming about the old days . . . Cynthia Ann and her son, Quanah; meeting the little baldy, Jesus, in a Texas *cantina*; cows dropping in their tracks on the Horsehead Trail; the thief, Abel Hagerty; losing my mule and $12,000 in gold; missing Mary Ann by two seconds; meeting Molly in Colorado; losing my first fortune; searching for the Palo Duro; bumping into the Adairs; fighting off Comanche; getting rich again . . . and I wonder how it all happened. I guess I'm just a lucky sonuvagun, that's all.

Author's note

Charlie Goodnight died aged ninety-three, in 1929, on his ranch, sixty-three years after blazing the Horsehead Trail. He left a town, a college and a legend in his name.

This is by no means a biography, but, based on the facts, a fictitious imagination of what life might have been like for the greatest of Texan cowboys in those far off days.

J.D